"Are you with Mad Dog?" Quot asked

Bolan tried to make some sense of the name as he prodded the man up the stairs. Mad Dog sounded like a code name, but for what?

The Vietnamese halted in the middle of the stairway, facing Bolan with a panic-stricken gaze. "How much are they paying you?" he demanded.

"I don't know what you're talking about." The warrior placed a hand on Quot's shoulder and spun him around, propelling him up the stairs to safety.

Bullets from a hidden gunner's weapon gouged chunks of wood from the stairway, racking the shaky structure with tremors.

As the Executioner sprinted up the steps, one of them gave way beneath him with a sickening wrench. Flailing his arms, Bolan caught the railing with his free hand and stopped his fall. He sent two rounds skipping over the hood of the Lincoln, driving the gunner to cover.

Flames darted out from beneath the Continental with a soft whoosh, spreading a blue-and-yellow torch that skated across the surface of the gasoline pouring from the ruptured tank.

Bolan was two feet from the doorway when the Lincoln exploded and tore the wooden structure out from beneath him.

MACK BOLAN®

The Executioner

#100 Blood Testament
#101 Eternal Triangle
#102 Split Image
#103 Assault on Rome
#104 Devil's Horn
#105 Countdown to Chaos
#106 Run to Ground
#107 American Nightmare
#108 Time to Kill
#109 Hong Kong Hit List
#110 Trojan Horse
#111 The Fiery Cross
#112 Blood of the Lion
#113 Vietnam Fallout
#114 Cold Judgment
#115 Circle of Steel
#116 The Killing Urge
#117 Vendetta in Venice
#118 Warrior's Revenge
#119 Line of Fire
#120 Border Sweep
#121 Twisted Path
#122 Desert Strike
#123 War Born
#124 Night Kill
#125 Dead Man's Tale
#126 Death Wind
#127 Kill Zone
#128 Sudan Slaughter
#129 Haitian Hit
#130 Dead Line
#131 Ice Wolf
#132 The Big Kill
#133 Blood Run
#134 White Line War
#135 Devil Force

Stony Man Doctrine
Terminal Velocity
Resurrection Day
Dirty War
Flight 741
Dead Easy
Sudden Death
Rogue Force
Tropic Heat
Fire in the Sky
Anvil of Hell
Flash Point
Flesh and Blood
Moving Target
Tightrope
Blowout
Blood Fever
Knockdown

DEVIL FORCE

A GOLD EAGLE BOOK FROM
WORLDWIDE®

TORONTO • NEW YORK • LONDON • PARIS
AMSTERDAM • STOCKHOLM • HAMBURG
ATHENS • MILAN • TOKYO • SYDNEY

First edition March 1990

ISBN 0-373-61135-8

Special thanks and acknowledgment to
Mel Odom for his contribution to this work.

Printed in U.S.A.

Revenge is a wild kind of Justice

—Francis Bacon
(1561-1626)

You find brutality everywhere you look. It's partly what makes the good things we do really stand out. Good and evil, you don't have one without the other. I try to draw a line around the innocents and fight fire with fire, hoping to maintain some kind of balance. Sometimes it's the best you can hope for.

—Mack Bolan

THE MACK BOLAN® LEGEND

Nothing less than a war could have fashioned the destiny of the man called Mack Bolan. Bolan earned the Executioner title in the jungle hell of Vietnam.

But this soldier also wore another name—Sergeant Mercy. He was so tagged because of the compassion he showed to wounded comrades-in-arms and Vietnamese civilians.

Mack Bolan's second tour of duty ended prematurely when he was given emergency leave to return home and bury his family, victims of the Mob. Then he declared a one-man war against the Mafia.

He confronted the Families head-on from coast to coast, and soon a hope of victory began to appear. But Bolan had broken society's every rule. That same society started gunning for this elusive warrior—to no avail.

So Bolan was offered amnesty to work within the system against terrorism. This time, as an employee of Uncle Sam, Bolan became Colonel John Phoenix. With a command center at Stony Man Farm in Virginia, he and his new allies—Able Team and Phoenix Force—waged relentless war on a new adversary: the KGB.

But when his one true love, April Rose, died at the hands of the Soviet terror machine, Bolan severed all ties with Establishment authority.

Now, after a lengthy lone-wolf struggle and much soul-searching, the Executioner has agreed to enter an "arm's-length" alliance with his government once more, reserving the right to pursue personal missions in his Everlasting War.

PROLOGUE

Cody Canada acted as if he hadn't heard the sound coming from his backyard. But all his senses were on full alert—as they had been for the past fifteen years. Ever since the Vietnam War ended, Canada had been looking over his shoulder, living with the knowledge that one day they would find him. He exhaled, almost a sigh of relief. He wasn't prepared to live like this any longer, in a way hoping they *had* found him.

All of his combat instincts returned; in fact they were never very far away. Canada didn't move from his position in the recliner. He even closed his hand around the sweating bottle of beer that sat on the floor next to the chair. He took a sip.

The sound came again, louder this time. Whoever was out there had closed the distance to the house. Canada could feel it, the way he used to feel the Cong breathing down his neck when he was on point.

Reaching down beside the recliner, he fisted the Ruger Blackhawk .44 out of the chair's big catchall. He flicked a switch at the side of the chair and the room plunged into darkness. Time to move.

Canada was out of his seat, his pulse hammering through his body. Just like Nam. This was no longer the house he had lived in for the past seven years. It was the jungle. He was no longer involved in the existence of Cody

Canada, the name he'd picked when he was fleshing out the identity he was going to use for the rest of his life. He had decided to bury the old self.

Clutching the big Magnum, he padded through the shadows of the dining room. The charcoal-gray warm-ups he wore absorbed the bleached-out light streaming in through the dining room window.

Squatting in the doorway leading to the kitchen, he tried to control his heartbeat the way he used to when he was on point. Shifting the gun to his other hand, he wiped his palm on his warm-up pants, then dragged a sleeve across his forehead, feeling the moisture plaster the cloth to his arm.

Silence.

He couldn't hear anything out there now.

But he was certain the intruder was still outside. He could feel the stranger's presence, as if he were in the room.

Pushing up from the squat, he crawled to the master bedroom. He moved to the window, unfastened the latch and slid the window up quietly, checking the shifting shadows in the backyard.

Still nothing.

Climbing over the sill he let his bare feet absorb the short drop as he landed in a flower bed. He melted into the side of the house, tucking the Magnum in close to his chest so that it couldn't be seen in silhouette.

The warm southern California night draped his body, evoking memories of a young soldier in a distant land. He paused at the corner of the house, letting his ears do the prelim probe. Sweat trickled down his spine.

Easing to his full height, he pressed his back against the house, trying to become another layer of siding. His right eye cleared the corner of the house only a split second ahead of the Blackhawk's muzzle. The yard was empty, deceptive, cloaked in moonlight. Just like the nighttime missions in the Parrot's Beak region of Nam. But he had survived that life, and others, as well. And he would survive this night, too. He'd left histories, not pleasant ones, for a lot of people, but he'd made a clean break with the past. The Major had seen to that.

A goldfish splashed in the small pond he'd built into the Japanese garden, interrupting his train of thought. He zigzagged across the yard to the shadows of a small wooden shed.

"Lawrence," a voice hissed.

Canada froze, letting the .44 follow the movements of his eyes. The name had been dead for fifteen years, dead and buried. He'd even seen the gravesite once—over ten years ago—knowing that the Major would have been pissed if he'd found out. But he had to go and see it, let the reality wash over him, see how much it really mattered.

"Lawrence."

Canada cursed himself for drifting off; his life depended on locating the intruder. Who had told the guy the name, and how much more did he know?

The thought made Canada uneasy, urging him into motion when he knew he should stay put and let the enemy come to him. He suddenly wished he had the team at his back. He and the Hawks, aka Satan's Backup, had taken on the whole NVA at times, it seemed, and had come out on top.

There had been a file on them near the end of the war, and the Major's Agency contact had said there was talk of shutting the team down permanently, taking no chances of garnering bad press regarding their activities in the jungle. But the Major had outfoxed them all, including the spooks who had unleashed them in the jungle in the first place. Under his guidance the team had made it out of Vietnam intact.

A new thought began to nibble at the edges of Canada's concentration. Maybe he shouldn't push the present situation. Just haul ass out of there and notify the Major that someone had penetrated their cover. But who? CIA? Military Intelligence? Someone from the other side?

It was one thing to pursue an enemy in the night on familiar ground and another to chase shadows when it seemed that the enemy knew more about you than they should.

Canada turned, prepared to jump the fence and escape across the neighboring backyards.

"Lawrence!" This time the voice was insistent, mocking.

Canada looked up, pinning the source now, realizing that it came from his rooftop. The goddamn figure stood in a relaxed manner, as if he had all the freakin' time in the world. Canada tried to see past the shadows clinging to the guy's face but couldn't.

Orange and yellow roses suddenly blossomed in the man's hands. As the slugs drilled into his chest, an incongruous thought crossed Canada's mind. Hell had come to suburbia.

The impact kicked him backward, and as he died, Canada could swear the gunner had a smile on his face.

VIRGIL WALLACE, ex-PFC of the United States Army and recently late of the ranks of 7 Eleven night clerks, limped through the grounds of Constitution Gardens. As usual, the amputated leg was giving him hell, but he refused to knuckle under to the pain. There was a vial of painkillers in a pocket of his fatigue jacket, but he refused to use the drug until he absolutely couldn't stand the pain anymore.

Which wouldn't be long now, he knew. It had been a constant part of his daily routine for more than a decade. Glancing up at the night sky, he noticed the gathering storm clouds. It would rain soon. That was the one thing the pain in his leg was good for. He always knew when to take a coat when he left the small, cluttered apartment he called home. At least that was what he called it for now.

Since he had lost the night clerk job and didn't have any promising opportunities, he figured he'd be moving back to the VA-sponsored living quarters until he got ready to face the street again.

Wallace turned up the collar of his jacket against the wind, shivering even though it wasn't that cold.

When he reached the Vietnam War Memorial he noticed that someone was already there.

Wallace brushed his long hair out of his eyes and tried to recognize the figure in the black trench coat. Maybe it was someone he knew. Wallace paused, letting the guy have some privacy with the lines of names, letting him touch base with the memories and ghosts, wondering if the guy in front of him was more successful at coping with life in the real world than he was.

At first glance Wallace thought so. There was a military shine on the black dress shoes, a certain set to the shoulders that bespoke self-discipline. But you never knew how somebody came back from the war or what kind of mental shape they were in until something tested them.

Wallace knew that his own inability to maintain interest in a job was a bigger problem than learning to use the artificial leg or dealing with the continual pain. Sure, people were willing to hire the vet, give the company a tax break and look good on the social calendar. But to care about the job? That was his problem.

He'd quit good jobs more times than he'd been fired. He just didn't care. Not about the paycheck or job security. He'd done all his caring in Vietnam, in the end finally surrendering to the scorn, the jeering when he'd returned—minus a leg. Even worse, he'd endured the venom of a thankless society while learning to walk on a painful steel-and-plastic leg.

No matter. This hunk of black granite meant something to Wallace. With thousands of others he'd come in November 1982 to see it dedicated and to trace his finger over the names of the guys he'd gone over with; guys who hadn't made it back.

He had started coming here at night a lot of years ago to avoid the curious people and the reporters who wanted to know what Vietnam had meant to him. He had developed the habit and stayed with it. It was always more peaceful at night.

Now America didn't seem to be afraid of the specter of Vietnam. Fifteen years had passed, time to start capitalizing on the situation. Oh, yes. TV series, big box-office movies, even maps and talk of tours. Forget the dead, the pain and suffering on both sides, the bloodshed. Look for the dollar value, man. Wallace shook his head sadly.

He figured the guy standing at the wall might be coping okay, but the ghosts were still there. The man had both hands on the monument, moving them back and forth like a blind person reading Braille. Then the guy took one hand off the wall and reached into his pocket. He withdrew something and brought it up near his face.

When Wallace heard the hiss he recognized the object as a can of spray paint.

"Hey, you!" Wallace yelled as he broke into an awkward jog. "Get the hell away from there, you son of a bitch!"

Without hurrying, the man dropped the spray can and casually walked away, glancing only briefly in Wallace's direction. Placing his hands on the wall to regain his balance, Wallace leaned forward, straining to see what damage had been done. Christ, what kind of maggot would do something like this? Why desecrate the names of the dead? There. A solid black line of paint. He wiped at it desperately with his sleeve, ignoring the biting pain in his leg.

Only one name had been painted over. Garry K. Lawrence. Wallace glanced over his shoulder, wondering what it had all been about. He wanted to ask the man in the trench coat, but the guy had vanished.

Only the black stain remained.

Rock music throbbed from speakers tucked into the corners of the spacious nightclub, providing explosive punctuations to the wild gyrations of the band that performed under the sweltering concert lights.

Mack Bolan threaded his way through the crowd, wishing his quarry had picked a different spot to roost. But it had taken almost eighteen hours of grueling recon over a large percentage of San Francisco to run Nguyen Tiep to ground, and he wasn't about to back off now.

A whirling, mirrored globe spun overhead, displaying tilted and splintered shadows over the chrome-and-red-leather interior of the nightclub. The band launched into another number, and the audience shouted and whistled its appreciation.

When Bolan had learned Tiep's whereabouts from his informant, he was reluctant to venture into the club, figuring he'd stick out in the crowd. Instead, the brown leather bomber jacket and dark jeans he wore fitted in surprisingly well. Only the Beretta 93-R he carried in shoulder leather would seem out of place.

The dance floor was huge, with a second-floor gallery surrounding the room. Only a sprinkling of tables occupied space on the bottom floor—most of the club's patrons preferred the booths upstairs.

The club was bigger than Bolan had anticipated when he received the call from Frankie Fabia, but it wasn't as posh as many of the clubs in the Bay Area. This was strictly a glitz-and-glamour business that catered to a young crowd.

Whining metallic riffs shrieked free of the lead guitarist's instrument as the lights over the stage flickered in a tempo that almost matched the spinning globe overhead. Tuning the music out, Bolan searched the sea of faces for Fabia or Tiep. Fragments of the phone conversation he'd had with Hal Brognola the day before stirred in his mind with the regularity of a ticking clock. Two men had been murdered—one an electrician in Los Angeles named "Cody Canada," the other named "Lester Stoddard," a field agent in the Justice Department. But both victims had had a note scrawled with another name pinned to his chest. And *those* names had been obliterated with spray paint from the Vietnam War Memorial in Washington, D.C. Both men, according to the incomplete records released by the CIA, had been assumed killed in action fifteen years earlier. The CIA was withholding additional information, pending an investigation.

So far Brognola hadn't been able to pry anything else free, including how a supposedly dead man who had worked with the CIA at the beginning of the Vietnam War in what was still classified operations could end up on the employment roster of the Justice Department for the past ten years.

The big Fed had been worried when he finally got a call through to Bolan, not knowing how far his department had been compromised or what the assassinations were leading up to. The papers were already full of what were being called the War Memorial murders.

Brognola also wasn't happy with Justice's profile these days. The new President's term was only a year old, and someone had gone out of his way to make the department look bad. As if Justice hadn't come under enough flack during the previous administration.

It would have been one thing, Brognola had said, if the CIA had offered to help clear the air, but Langley was playing this one close to the vest. Officially there was no CIA interest in the assassinations. Unofficially Brognola could feel pressure building up in Wonderland as everyone scurried around trying to cover their collective butts before the next body dropped. He had felt certain of that even before he found a bug in his office only two days earlier. A sweep conducted the same day had turned up three more in different nerve centers of Justice. So far Brognola hadn't brought the bugs to the attention of the CIA director, feeling it would only muddy the waters and make a real investigation that much harder.

Cody Canada, real name Garry Lawrence, had been found shot dead in his backyard the previous week. Lester Stoddard, real name William Anselm, was executed in a bar three days ago in front of more than twenty witnesses who couldn't nail down an accurate description of the killer between them. The hit had gone down too quickly. Which meant the hitter was someone who knew the habits of the men he was stalking.

The time factor involved between hits suggested to Bolan that only one man or a small team was involved in the assassinations. Apparently whoever was doing the killing had all the information he—or they—needed to reach out and tag the targets at any time. But why let the rest of the men on the hit list know what was going on? Why mark the Wall?

It was possible that not all of the assassin's targets could be trailed as easily as the first two. But what made the hunter believe he could flush his birds from their hiding places? If these men had worked for the CIA during the Vietnam War, they were as accustomed to being the hunted as they were to being the hunters.

Bolan brushed the thoughts away as he found Fabia seated at a small table near the bar. A half-dozen empty glasses lined the tabletop, each with a tiny umbrella sunk in its depths. Choosing the path of least resistance, Bolan made his way toward the man, keeping an arm over the Beretta so that if someone accidently bumped into him the hard outlines of the weapon wouldn't be detected.

"What have you got, Frankie?" Bolan asked as he took a seat at the table.

Fabia was six-three, Bolan's height, but without his weight, and possessed a nervousness that complemented his rail-thin physique. He was part of the young Mafia trying to get its roots into the North Beach area and had been easily impressed by the ace of spades Bolan had shown him earlier that morning. His dark hair was long and carefully groomed, allowing him to fit in with the rock crowd at the club or with the image maintained by the newest Mafia don in San Francisco.

"Christ, Omega," Fabia said as he brushed his spilled drink from his lap, "I didn't even see you coming."

Bolan remained silent, thinking his impassiveness would have been more threatening if they had been somewhere else besides the club. Still, it was a role the Mafia guy would have expected from a Black Ace, and the playing card had told Fabia that was what Bolan was.

Fabia blotted his pants with a handful of napkins, cursing softly.

"Frankie..." Bolan let a note of impatience creep into his voice, which wasn't just part of the character he was playing. Some of it was from the heart and soul. He'd been up the past twenty-seven hours trying to get a fix on the killings.

"Yeah, I'm sorry, Omega, you just startled me. That's all."

"Tiep," Bolan reminded.

"Yeah, sure, I got him. Just like I told you I would. You came to the right guy for this assignment, Omega. You might remember that to the right ears later, if you know what I mean."

"Tiep."

Fabia nodded. "Behind you. Three tables back behind the wall. He's got two guys with him."

Bolan leaned back in his chair as if to attract the attention of a passing cocktail waitress. The move also brought Tiep and his men into view for a moment.

Tiep matched the photo in the mug file Bolan had leafed through at the San Francisco Police Department that morning before making the meet with Fabia. According to the file, Tiep had been arrested a number of times on drug trafficking charges, but the witnesses had a habit of disappearing or changing their minds about who they saw. Undercover cops sent to infiltrate Tiep's network usually didn't come back.

The SFPD's files only began in 1976 when Tiep had first been arrested for distribution, but Bolan's intel concerning the man went back farther. All the way back to Vietnam. The Executioner hadn't come in contact with Tiep during his tours, but there had been rumors concerning the man before and after the war. Tiep had been second-in-command of a cocaine operation in Vietnam, working the fields with the blessing of the CIA, who used him and his organization to ferret out intel about the NVA. Tiep and his boss had worked both sides of the fence. Then the

United States pulled out of the conflict and the duo had nowhere to go except the land of opportunity.

Tiep wasn't the brains behind the operation, only a rung on the ladder. Bolan's real target was the man who kept Tiep organized and running on schedule. The SFPD's files hadn't even mentioned Gung Quot's name. Bolan was sure the CIA kept a file on Quot, just as he was equally sure the CIA would turn down Brognola's request for information.

"You never did say what you wanted with this guy, Omega," Fabia said.

Bolan glanced at the man. "That's right," he said through a mirthless smile. "I didn't."

Fabia shrugged uncomfortably. "There's a lot of people wondering what you're doing here in town. I mean, you're an Ace. That kind of gets people a little on edge, you know."

Bolan knew, which was why he wanted to move fast on this operation. Black Aces were a power unto themselves in the Mafia. If an Ace chose to execute a capo, the Ace could do it without any repercussions. If Tiep hadn't turned up in the next few hours, Omega would have had to fade, anyway. An Ace didn't drop onto the scene to stand around twiddling his thumbs.

Fabia flinched from Bolan's granite stare. "No disrespect intended, Omega, but if you've got trouble with Tiep, Carm wanted me to let you know he could take care of it for you."

Bolan smiled easier this time, but knew it wouldn't relax Fabia because the man didn't know how far he had transgressed on an Ace's personal turf. "Carm doesn't think I can take care of this myself, Frankie?"

"No, no, not that." Fabia stuck a finger down the collar of his shirt to loosen his tie. "Carm's young, just coming into his own, you know. He didn't think anything like that. He just wants to do you a favor. If that's possible."

"Carm DiCarlo isn't so young that he doesn't know how to show respect, Frankie," Bolan replied. "You tell him I think he's getting a little like Pinocchio, and it would be better if he kept his nose in his own business."

"Yes, sir."

Bolan could see the dark flush of embarrassment on Fabia's face even in the dimly lit club.

The waitress brought their drinks and plunked them on the table without a word. Bolan sipped the screwdriver and checked on Tiep. The man hadn't moved. "You did a good job finding these guys," he told Fabia.

"Thanks."

"What does DiCarlo know about Tiep?"

"Not a lot. You probably got more on Tiep than Carm does."

"Pretend I don't know anything, Frankie."

Fabia shrugged and shuffled his glass from hand to hand. "We know he moves crack almost by the boxcar load. At least that's what some of the local deals believe. They also say he has his own source coming from somewhere in Vietnam, that the Communist government has some kind of special deal with him to get him the stuff cheap as long as he makes them his only connection."

Bolan nodded. The SFPD didn't have any of this in their files, but it dovetailed with his personal intel. He wasn't surprised to learn the DiCarlo organization was aware of it, though. Tiep and Quot represented the competition, and the Mafia always kept close tabs on the competition.

"He's got a big network of suppliers, too, but they work the Chinatown district mostly. Carm's had his eye on Tiep ever since he stepped into office, but Tiep keeps his fingers in his own pies and doesn't cross over into our territory. Still, Carm is anxious, you know, about Tiep thinking it'd be okay to move in now since Carm's the new kid on the block."

"And maybe Carm's a little hungry, too," Bolan suggested. "Maybe he's thinking about how much business there is to be had in Chinatown and about how nobody's had the balls to challenge Tiep lately."

"Maybe. Like I said, Carm's young. Got a lot of growing up to do. His old man died on him too soon and never got around to filling Carm in on a lot of the facts of life. It seems he doesn't remember the wars we fought with the Vietnamese over the territory during the early eighties, or the blood that was shed until Mr. DiCarlo and Tiep figured out an arrangement that suited everybody concerned."

"Tiep's always been in charge of things here?"

"As far as I know. Every now and then you hear this little rumor, like maybe Tiep isn't the top dog of the organization, that somebody else in pulling his strings."

Interest flared inside Bolan, but he was careful to keep it from his face. "These rumors mention any names?"

Fabia shook his head. "No. Anybody who gets that close to Tiep usually ends up as fish bait. But there's been a couple of times that Tiep looked like he was going down for a heavy number and somebody with a lot of bread and a lot of grease found some slack in the system. I mean, Christ, Mr. DiCarlo, Carm's old man, was in on one of the busts on Tiep. We had cops inside the DEA that Mr. D. bankrolled to help plant the evidence. This was all before anyone realized some ground rules were going to have to be ironed out. Anyway, the bust was made, the evidence was tagged and Tiep was booked. Twenty-four hours later Tiep was on the street, confident and cocky as hell. A few days later at the inquest the charges were dropped. Except for the carrying of a concealed weapon. Seems the cocaine found in Tiep's possession had turned into milk sugar when nobody was looking.'' Fabia paused to light a cigarette.

When the lighter sparked to life, Bolan could see the abject fear on the man's face.

Fabia snapped the lighter shut and put it away. ''About two weeks later somebody hit the DEA cops Mr. D. had bought off. Tiep had flowers sent to the funerals. Within the next year Carm's dad and Tiep reached an agreement. I was there, and I had the same feeling running through my gut then that I got now. That little slant-eyed son of a bitch is death to mess with, Omega. Even Mr. DiCarlo had to admit that in the end. And he's got some kind of shadow running interference for him when things get tight.''

''You're wrong about that, Frankie,'' Bolan said. ''I know about the guy Tiep works for.''

''You must be fucking psychic then, because I know guys who've been turning over rocks from here to D.C. trying to get the dirt on this guy. Closest they ever came, I swear on my mother's grave you aren't gonna believe this shit, but the closest they ever came was some file lost in CIA records.''

Bolan could believe it because it was that tie that had brought him to San Francisco. ''What did these guys turn up?''

''What did they turn up? Shit, no disrespect, Omega, but haven't you been listening? Those guys didn't turn up anything. That's why Mr. D. cut the deal. You can't touch Tiep or the guy behind him.''

Bolan didn't say anything. Tiep and his two companions still hadn't moved. A blond girl had separated from the crowd on the dance floor and was talking animatedly with Tiep.

"There's torpedos and icemen on the street who won't touch this bastard," Fabia said. "Even if they did get through the guys who are with him constantly and did manage to hit Tiep, his men would hit them and their families. These guys got no class at all. It's one thing to ax a guy you got business with, but you stay away from his family." Fabia exhaled a long stream of smoke. "The reason I'm telling you this, Omega, is because I don't know what your business here is or what you've been told about Tiep and his organization. What I'm giving you is the straight goods. I was there. I saw the blood it cost to kind of find a balance for things. I shed a little of it myself once. I just want you to know, Ace or no Ace, if you're planning on tangling with Tiep, I want to be dealt out."

Bolan studied the man's features, reading fear in the pinched nostrils and the white spots on his forehead above his eyes. Frank Fabia was supposed to be one of the old DiCarlo regime's most stand-up wise guys, a man who'd stand at your side no matter how rough the going got. Which was why Bolan, as Black Ace Omega, had connected with Carm DiCarlo's organization and demanded Fabia be assigned to him to investigate Tiep. Fabia was also one of the few who had been around long enough to see Tiep become entrenched in San Francisco's drug culture, who would have some knowledge Bolan could use in taking Tiep down. It had taken a lot of courage for Fabia to demand out.

"It's no problem, Frankie," Bolan said easily. "You're dealt out. This is my show now. I just needed you to find the guy for me."

Fabia nodded. "I appreciate that, Omega. You'll never guess how much. So, if there's nothing else, I'm gonna go find a hole and pull it in after me. If you plan on torching this guy, you don't have to stay around while everything goes to hell. I do, and I intend to keep my ass intact."

"Don't worry about things here, Frankie," Bolan said. "What goes down here tonight will never touch the Family or Carm. I've got an angle that'll have everybody looking somewhere else."

Fabia downed the remainder of his drink and dropped his cigarette into the glass. There was no humor in his smile. "Yeah, well, we'll see." He started to walk away, then turned back. "One other thing."

Bolan raised an eyebrow.

"Tiep wears an ankle gun. Thought you'd want to know."

"Thanks."

Fabia waved it away and disappeared into the crowd of dancers.

Bolan sipped the screwdriver and waited, turning things over in his mind, wondering if he was pursuing a cold trail. The blonde was still talking to Tiep, kneeling by the booth with her elbow on the tabletop. The warrior tried to get a fix on her age and figured her for no more than early twenties. Tiep was easily twice that.

Tiep's smile was broad and indulgent. Gold-encrusted gems sparkled on his fingers as he moved them in time to the music. His white suit was immaculate, making him stand out against the club's dark decor and the gray suits of his bodyguards.

As Bolan watched his quarry, he focused on the worry that had been in Brognola's voice during the call yesterday, and turned over in his mind what he'd been told. The two murdered men had covers that had provided them with more or less complete lives since the war. But who had locked the covers into place? And why? If they hadn't died fifteen years ago, who had? Why was that kept secret?

Someone obviously wanted them dead, but who had pulled the trigger? What difference did it make fifteen years after the war? Why was the CIA monitoring what was happening in the Justice Department?

Brognola had mentioned that both men's records—the few the CIA were willing to relinquish—bore the same date of death, which sounded like a busted play the Agency had put together near the end of the war. If the CIA had been behind the cover-up, the Agency would have been breaking its butt right now trying to keep the story dead, doing its utmost to get the surviving men out of sight. Yet, according to Brognola's sources, Langley seemed as off balance as anyone, waiting for the next body to drop.

Bolan was sure there would be more. Whoever had pulled the trigger on Canada and Stoddard had wanted news of the kills to hit the papers. That was why the Vietnam War Memorial had been spray-painted: to let the others know they were being stalked. But how many others?

The warrior was counting on Gung Quot to know the answer to that one. Otherwise he had wasted the past eighteen hours.

Quot had been a top Vietnamese liaison for the CIA at the beginning of the war. Bolan had heard of Quot from the days he'd spent working with Colonel Robert McFee. McFee had been a Military Intelligence liaison with the CIA at the same time Quot had been operating, as well as heading up some of Bolan's operations with PenTeam Able. The colonel was still involved with the search for MIAs and the future of the Meo, just as he had been the last time Bolan had seen him, but now he was doing it from a desk in D.C. and not the jungle. It had been McFee who had given Bolan the intel concerning Quot's presence in San Francisco. The Agency still kept tabs on certain key ex-personnel. McFee kept personal tabs on even more.

If there was any one man who might be able to make some sense of the names of the dead men, Bolan figured it would be Quot. Perhaps not much, but definitely more than Brognola would be able to ferret out of Langley.

According to McFee, the Agency knew Quot was running the crack action in San Francisco's Chinatown but had declined to pass on the information to bring him down. McFee had gone on to say, dryly, that the main reason for the Agency's reluctance was due to the fact that Quot was still harvesting from the fields the CIA had helped him establish in Vietnam, and the brass didn't want to risk the national exposure. If the Agency set the wheels in motion to bust Quot and succeeded, it would not only acquire a lot of bad press, but would create a void that would fill itself naturally with someone equally as bad. With Quot in place the CIA still had someone to turn to for select "work" in other countries that wouldn't track directly back to them.

McFee had seemed surprised by the information when Bolan got back to him.

Bolan wasn't. McFee had only touched base with the CIA concerning military matters in a country the United States had been at war with. The Executioner had crossed the tangled paths the Agency left scattered around the globe several times.

The blonde stood up, waving goodbye.

Tiep leaned forward and watched her go, saying something that provoked laughter in his companions. Then he slid out of the booth and made his way to the men's room, his bodyguards falling into step behind him.

Feeling the pulse of adrenaline beat inside his temples, Bolan left his table and trailed in their wake, opening his jacket to allow easier access to the 93-R. He pushed through the crowd, drawing a few scathing remarks from the jostled dancers, keeping Tiep in view over the bobbing and jerking heads.

Tiep paused at the door to the men's room as two young men walked out. One of the bodyguards entered first, then waved an all-clear.

Bolan noted the reflexive security measure, noticing how the move had seemed to be more protocol than professional. Tiep had been enjoying the good life too long, the Executioner thought as he cut the distance to his quarry. Even the threat of Carmine DiCarlo's newly acquired power wasn't being treated as a possible danger.

Still, it didn't make the men any less dangerous, and Bolan knew that, too.

At the long row of sinks inside, two yuppies were conducting a business transaction concerning a vial of coke. Another guy was busy trying to revive a fifty-dollar hairstyle and wasn't having much success. Tiep and his bodyguards had blocked off the last stall. Both men were relaxed, smoking cigarettes.

The guy with the dead hairstyle left. The two involved in the drug deal seemed to be haggling over the money. Bolan stepped to the last sink out of the bodyguards' sight and turned the water on. Aware that someone else might walk through the door at any time, he reached inside his jacket and pulled out his phony Justice ID. Holding his finger to his lips, he flashed it at the yuppies and watched their faces turn white. They couldn't see the badge to know what it was, but the general idea was enough. Bolan waved them through the door.

Tiep kept up a running conversation with his bodyguards in Vietnamese as he relieved himself. Most of his comments had to do with the blonde who had joined them at their table. Tiep was willing to bet with one of the bodyguards that he would take her home.

Glancing in the mirror as he let the water run, Bolan noticed that one of the bodyguards watched the yuppies' departure with increasing interest. When he started to call for his partner's attention, the warrior reached for the Beretta.

Whirling around the first stall, Bolan dropped the 93-R into target acquisition and triggered a silenced 3-round burst that punched 9 mm death into one of the guards. The surviving man yelled a warning to Tiep as he freed a Detonics .45 from its shoulder holster and squeezed the trigger. The bullet went high, smashing into the fluorescent lights over Bolan's head. Glass splinters showered to the floor as the familiar cloying odor of the neon dust tightened the Executioner's lungs. His next 3-round burst spiked the bodyguard through the chest, knocking him back against the wall.

Bolan could see the man screaming, but couldn't hear anything since the first booming detonation of the Detonics. He saw the muzzle-flash of the next shot as a fist-size hole appeared in the privacy wall next to him and a mirror collapsed in his peripheral vision. He stroked the Beretta's trigger again, watching the point of the bodyguard's chin implode.

Moving forward, knowing the numbers were falling rapidly, Bolan slammed into the stall door as Tiep tried to rush out. His greater weight hurled the Vietnamese back against the toilet. He shoved the sprung door to one side, deflecting Tiep's attempt to bring up a stainless-steel Heckler & Koch. The Executioner tightened his left hand into a fist and delivered two short jabs into Tiep's face, which split the skin over the man's cheekbones. Blood flowed copiously from Tiep's nose and mouth.

The injured man's high-pitched screech penetrated the dulled cotton numbness that had filled Bolan's ears. "You son of a bitch!" the man screamed, spitting blood. "You're dead. Dead! Do you understand me?"

Then Tiep hawked a mouthful of bloody spittle at Bolan's face and leaped for the top of the privacy wall, struggling to get a leg over.

Bolan grabbed the back of Tiep's collar and yanked the man back, the Beretta's muzzle flush against the crack broker's cheek. "We're going to talk," the Executioner said in Vietnamese. "Just you and me."

"I'm not talking to anybody!" Tiep yelled. "I want my lawyer!"

Bolan dragged the resisting man out of the stall and forced him to take a good look at one of the dead bodyguards. "Do you think a lawyer's going to do this guy much good?"

"Who are you looking for?" Tiep demanded just as the door to the men's room opened.

"What the hell's going on here?" a redheaded young Atlas roared as he started to cross the threshold. He was one of the matched pair of young security guards Bolan had noticed at the club's door. When the kid saw the blood on the walls, his face blanched and he looked as if he were about to be sick.

"Out!" Bolan ordered.

The guy vanished.

Without warning Tiep twisted in Bolan's grasp and reached for his ankle.

With lighting reflexes the Executioner shoved the man's face to the floor, and before Tiep could recover, stripped off the hidden gun and pitched it into the toilet.

"Get up," Bolan ordered, motioning with the Beretta. Holding Tiep by the scruff of the neck, he guided the man to his feet. He retrieved a pair of plastic handcuffs from inside his jacket and cuffed his captive's hands behind him.

One of Tiep's eyes was swollen shut, and his bottom lip puffed out like bloated leech. "You aren't a cop," Tiep said. "A cop in this town would know better than to try to pull this kind of shit. You work for Carmine DiCarlo, don't you?" His open eye glared belligerence, dark and hostile.

"No," Bolan replied, pushing Tiep toward the door. He tucked the 93-R under his jacket but kept his hand on it. "I don't work for anybody you know."

"This is the kind of stunt DiCarlo would pull."

"DiCarlo doesn't have anybody with enough nerve to pull this stunt," Bolan growled into the man's ear. He maintained his hold on the cuffs. "Remember? You and Quot made sure of that."

Tiep stumbled at the mention of Quot's name. He looked over his shoulder at Bolan, new fear dawning in the muddy brown depths of his eye.

The nightclub crowd cleared the way for Bolan and his prisoner, the rock band standing onstage silently. The sound of approaching sirens shrilled outside.

"Yeah," Bolan continued as they stepped outside into the night, "I know about Quot and I know about the loose relationship he maintains with some of the old guard at the Agency. The only thing I need to know is where he is now. You're going to help me with that." He stopped in the club's parking lot beside a black 1965 Chevy SuperSport, then motioned Tiep inside with the Beretta.

The sirens sounded closer.

"You're crazy, man," Tiep mumbled. "I'm not telling you a goddamn thing."

Bolan stepped closer, letting his size intimidate the smaller man. His voice remained soft, understated. "I'm not a cop, Tiep, and I'm not with Carm DiCarlo. I'm not anybody you know. If I put a bullet through your head right now, nobody will be able to touch me."

Tiep blinked furiously, and Bolan could almost see the options sorting themselves out in the man's mind. "How do I know you won't kill me when I tell you?"

"You've got my word."

"Your word?" Tiep didn't even try to hide his derision. "Since when does the Agency keep its word?"

"That's as good as it gets," Bolan said, keeping his face impassive. The muzzle of the Beretta never wavered.

The police cruisers sounded mere blocks away now.

"Time's up," Bolan said. He kept his face still and hard, smelling the fear his prisoner exuded. "Either we talk or I save myself the trouble of carrying you around."

Tiep's facade shattered, and he took a shuddering breath. "Let's go."

Bolan opened the door of the Chevy and pushed Tiep inside. A patrol car screeched into the street as Bolan hit the Chevy's ignition. He kept the Beretta trained on Tiep's midsection as he guided the vehicle onto the street behind the nightclub, keeping his lights off until he was in the flow of traffic.

The Warrior hoped his opening play would generate another lead for him to follow. Gung Quot's relationship with the CIA had been an obtuse angle to approach the questions of why the dead men had been listed as killed in action, and why they had been assassinated fifteen years later. But the angle had appealed to the Executioner because Quot was old business with the Agency. Just as the murdered men had been. Bolan knew secrets never went away; they always left a mark, as Tiep had proved. The man had instantly jumped to the conclusion that Bolan was CIA. And the Warrior wanted to know why the jump in logic had been so easy. By rattling every cage he could get his hands on, Bolan figured he'd shake something loose from the facelift the Agency had performed on whatever operation had gone sour fifteen years earlier.

He'd shake something loose.

Or someone.

2

Detective Sergeant Whit Talbot of the San Francisco Police Department sighed tiredly as he went over his report for the third time. He shifted his weight in the hard swivel chair, trying to find relief for his aching back. It was no use.

Girlish laughter drew his attention from the paperwork. The two young prostitutes Raymond had picked up in the Tenderloin seemed to be enjoying themselves as they sat with the plainclothes detective at his desk. One woman was a blonde, one a brunette, and both were dressed as suggestively as possible.

For a moment Talbot envied Alex Raymond's easy camaraderie with the hookers. Raymond was still young—seasoned, to be sure, but still naive about some aspects of life—like the fact that everybody got old and crotchety, he thought sourly as he flipped another page over. Raymond could still appreciate the beauty of the two girls he was booking and not see the worn-out rejects they would become in a handful of years. If they weren't dead by then.

Heaving another deep sigh, Talbot forced himself to his feet and made his way across the squad room to the dented coffeepot. He poured a cup, blinking at the dryness in his eyes and wishing for once that he could leave the damn report alone and just go home. The problem was, he hated loose ends. Everything had to be neat and tidy before he relinquished it. At first, that desire for perfection had been a boon to his career, had helped a twelve-year veteran patrolman make the grade to detective when he figured out an angle on the murder of a big businessman that none of the detectives assigned to the case had considered. Now it was no longer a desire. It was part of the mechanical process of his job. No longer did the chief think the extra care was something special about Detective Sergeant Talbot; now it was expected. He saw to it that Talbot caught the squeals that required a keen, incisive mind and somebody who'd put the time in on the case to develop it.

That desire for perfection was no longer a boon to his career. Now it kept him up at nights and was putting gray in his hair. He yawned and sipped the coffee, moving over to one of the open windows to drink in the night air rolling in from the Bay.

Maybe he ought to really consider walking away from the police force, become a deputy in the Sheriff's Department or something. He grinned at his reflection at the thought, watching the middle-aged black man with gray staining his mustache and shadowing his temples grin back.

"Hey, Whit!"

Talbot turned to look at Raymond, who was pecking industriously at the old Underwood on his desk. The girls had apparently been taken away while he was enjoying his bit of middle-aged depression. "Yeah?"

"How many *e*'s are there in *separate*?" Raymond had a cigarette tucked behind one ear and blew a bubble as he waited.

"Two," Talbot replied.

A moment later Raymond leaned back in the chair and said, "You know, that doesn't look right."

"What doesn't look right?"

"*Separate*."

"What doesn't look right about it?"

"It looks like it's got too many *e*'s."

Talbot chuckled and wrapped a big hand under his chin. "How'd you spell it, Alex?"

"S-E-P-E-R-A-T-E."

"How many *e*'s you got there?"

Raymond counted them. "Three." He wrinkled his face, looking like a high school kid trying to figure out how he got such a low grade on a term paper. "Where the hell did that extra *e* come from?"

The young detective applied a liberal dose of Liquid Paper to the arrest sheet, popping his gum noisily. "Did you hear that squeal Barnes and Keefer caught earlier?"

"No." Talbot stared out the window again, wondering if he'd be able to give his report just one more read, then get the hell home. His need for perfection had also cost him a marriage early on in his career. Thankfully Mandy was more her own person than Claire had been. Of course, Mandy being Mandy had required a few compromises on both sides, too. Mandy Brooks was ten years younger than Talbot, and looked ten years younger than that. Talbot figured most people guessed he was Mandy's father when they went out together. She was also a damn good bartender, which was how they met.

"Yeah, they got a call on a double homicide at that new nightclub on Union Street."

"The one with all the glitter inside?" Talbot felt his heart rate speed up.

"Yeah, that's the one. Mandy tends bar near there, doesn't she?"

"Yeah." Talbot recrossed the squad room and sat back at his desk, telling himself that nothing had happened to Mandy. Still, it wouldn't be totally out of line to give her a call. He checked his watch. Yeah, maybe it would. Christ, how did it get to be half past eight so fast? Mandy would be in full swing now, dealing with the high rollers at the club where she tended bar, and she didn't like being interrupted. She was a lady who took her work seriously, which had suited Talbot at first but now seemed to irritate him at times. He took his hand from the phone.

Raymond resumed pounding the typewriter keys. "Turns out the guys who got aced were a couple of Nguyen Tiep's bodyguards."

"Tiep's bodyguards," Talbot echoed. "You sure it was Tiep's guys who got hit?"

"Yeah. I was there when Keefer took the squeal. The uniforms were as excited as hell. Here we been spending years trying to get the goods on these guys, and somebody does us a favor and offs them."

Leaning back in his chair, Talbot laced his fingers behind his head and remembered the big man from the Justice Department who had dropped by to introduce himself that morning. He had pulled the Tiep file for the guy. He rustled through the pages of his report until he found the index card on which he'd written the Justice agent's name: Belasko, Michael, Special Agent, Justice. He tapped the card with a long forefinger, turning the name over in his mind. He still didn't get a feeling for anything behind the name, but there was plenty he'd gotten from the man. Loose ends. God, how he hated them. What were the chances that a big-time Justice agent would blow into town the same day two of Nguyen Tiep's bodyguards would get killed in the bathroom of a nightclub?

"Poetic justice," Raymond said. "Here we were looking to nail these clowns for crack trafficking, and now we're gonna be spending the city's money trying to find the people who did humanity a favor. Ought to give the guy who did it the Nobel Peace Prize instead of throwing him in the slammer."

"The guy?" Talbot's interest was piqued despite his wishing he could just blow it off and walk away. It wasn't his squeal, damn it.

"One guy."

Talbot tapped the index card again. "What about witnesses?"

"Dozens of them, Whit. The nightclub was filled."

"What about Tiep?"

"The guy who dusted the bodyguards took Tiep out with him when he left."

"Have they found Tiep's body yet?"

"No, but the uniforms are running the streets looking for it. Personally I think we'll find the guy floating in the Bay in the morning."

Talbot laced his fingers behind his head again. "No. If this was intended as a hit, the guy would have dropped the hammer on Tiep in the nightclub."

"You're beginning to get that look on your face the chief loves," Raymond said, leaning backward over the swivel chair.

"What kind of ID did the crowd get on the hitter?"

"Big guy, moved quick. When he took Tiep out, Tiep was cuffed. Most of the people watching thought he was a cop."

"White?"

"Yeah."

"Nobody saw what this guy left in?"

Raymond shrugged. "Beats the hell out of me, Sarge. I'm not working the case. I listened long enough to get my jollies when the squeal came in. Tiep's been waiting to get his a long time."

Talbot nodded. He had been in uniform the last time the DEA had tried to pin a drug charge on the Vietnamese and could still remember what had happened to one of the DEA agents and his family. The hit on Tiep tonight didn't make sense. Who would have pulled it off? Carmine DiCarlo didn't have the backing for it yet, even if he decided to challenge Tiep's rule over the Chinatown crack trade. What kind of guy would figure on taking Tiep's bodyguards out in a public place and walking away with Tiep as the door prize?

"It's kind of odd, don't you think?" Raymond asked.

"What?" Talbot asked mechanically.

"That Justice guy asking about Tiep on the same day somebody whacks Tiep's bodyguards. Real poetic justice."

"The term is *irony*," Talbot said reflexively. He'd let Raymond's incorrect terminology pass earlier because he'd conditioned himself to overlook most of what the younger man said unless it applied to work. Now his mind was occupied with the day's events, and he hadn't been able to stop himself.

Raymond didn't seem to be bothered by the correction. "Yeah, well, I got some more irony for you."

Talbot looked at him. "What's that?"

"Your Justice guy is back." Raymond made a gun of his forefinger and thumb, then pulled the trigger in the direction of the squad room doors.

Talbot worked his swivel chair to face in the direction of the doors. The squad room was small and cramped, with a close, stale smell not even the springtime could wash away. Paperwork littered most of the half-dozen desks that filled the room, each with its own Underwood and gooseneck lamp.

The detective watched the new arrival with interest, tapping the index card a final time before sliding it out of sight. Mike Belasko was a big man and moved with the grace of a quick guard, tight and controlled. His brown bomber jacket was zipped at the bottom but was loose enough to conceal the hardware underneath. He wore a black baseball cap bearing a Jack Daniel's logo, which gave him a just-one-of-the-guys look that hadn't drawn a second glance from the detectives on the early shift.

"You're keeping late hours tonight, Sergeant," Belasko said in a friendly tone.

"You look like you're putting in a few long ones yourself, Agent Belasko."

"Mind if I have a seat?"

Talbot waved to Raymond's chair, interested in spite of his intentions to the contrary. If this guy had waltzed into the nightclub and offed Tiep's bodyguards, would he be collected enough to be sitting in a squad room now? Mentally the detective cursed his curiosity.

"I got a fresh pot of coffee on," Raymond called from the other side of the room.

Bolan nodded and said thanks.

"You got a reason for this visit," Talbot asked, "or are you just passing through?"

Bolan's grin was easy, natural. "Actually, I came back for some more help."

Talbot monitored his voice, keeping it flat and neutral. "Yeah, I can see where Tiep getting killed might complicate your investigation a little."

"I wasn't aware Tiep had been killed," Bolan replied. "I caught a report on the radio that said he'd been abducted, but nothing was said about his being dead."

"They haven't found Tiep's body yet," Talbot replied, leaning forward to place his elbows on the desk. The man from Justice didn't move or indicate in any way that he felt his space was being invaded. It was a cheap trick at best,

Talbot decided, useful only on people who had something to hide and weren't very good at hiding it. "Maybe I'm being premature."

"Maybe you are," Bolan agreed. "You might even find that Tiep's willing to be a little more talkative to the right people after an experience like this."

Talbot wondered if there had been a double meaning to Belasko's words, then dismissed the thought. The guy was too laid-back to try rousting without more to go on than a gut feeling.

"Coffee's done," Raymond announced. "How do you like yours, Belasko?"

"Black."

As the man from Justice leaned forward to accept the proffered paper cup, Talbot caught a glimpse of the hardware concealed beneath his bomber jacket, recognizing it as some bastardized type of Beretta that wouldn't be carried by a uniform or a plainclothes detective. He filed the information away for later reference.

"Guess you're out of a job, huh?" Raymond asked as he leaned against the edge of his desk.

"Tiep wasn't the only reason I came to town," Bolan said easily, not taking his eyes from Talbot.

Talbot considered the Justice man's words. From the way Belasko had acted that morning, Tiep had been the major concern and focus of whatever investigation had brought him to San Francisco. The detective had politely shown his curiosity and Belasko had politely shown his disinclination to satisfy it. So what had changed? Besides Tiep's disappearance? Talbot flicked a pointed glance at the younger detective. "Don't you have a report to file, Alex? I mean, now that you've got *separate* spelled correctly."

Taking the hint, Raymond gathered his arrest sheet and moved out with a small salute.

Talbot looked back at the Justice agent. "What can I do for you?"

Bolan set his coffee cup down and removed a small notepad from an inside jacket pocket. "I need to know if you can get a schematic on the building at that address."

Taking the notepad, Talbot glanced at the address, saying, "I don't suppose I could ask why you wanted something like that."

"You could ask," Bolan replied. "It's just that I couldn't say."

Talbot nodded and dropped the notepad onto his desk. The address was written in a precise, neat hand, as no-nonsense as the big man sitting in front of him. "What kind of schematic do you want?"

"General layout, the electrical lines, water, plumbing."

"What about the real estate history?"

"That's not necessary."

"You know where this building is?"

"I drove by there."

"So you know it's in the Bay area near Chinatown?"

Bolan nodded.

"And you can't tell me what this has to do with Tiep?"

"No. If getting those schematics is going to be a problem," Bolan continued, "I can wait until morning and get a section chief to lean on somebody in the courthouse."

Talbot reached for the phone. "No, it's no problem. I've got a friend who can get her hands on the schematics in an hour or so."

"And whatever building permits have been issued for the site lately."

"Right." Talbot punched the number from memory, watching the Justice agent sip the coffee. "Sherry, it's

Whit, babe. I've got an address I need schematics on." He read the address off the notepad. "Yeah, yeah, specs, building permits, the whole song and dance. Morning? Sorry, honey, I've got a man waiting to move on this now. An hour? Good enough." He put the phone away. "That suit you?"

"Yeah. Thanks, Sergeant."

"Don't mention it." Talbot noticed the little scars on the agent's jawline. The doctor had done a good job, but the marks still indicated plastic surgery to somebody in the know. In the detective's mind those little scars of Belasko's turned into tiny question marks. "Guess you've got yourself an hour to kill, ace."

Bolan shook his head and drained his coffee cup. "Not really. I've got a few more rocks to turn over between now and then." He stood. "Who do I need to see about the schematics when I come back?"

Easing back against the swivel chair, Talbot laced his fingers behind his head. "Me."

The warrior grinned. "Sounds like your bucking for a promotion, Sergeant."

"I'm just a curious man living in a world full of puzzles, Agent Belasko. I tend to pick and pry and push until I can make some kind of sense of them. I've got a few loose ends here to nudge around before I call it a night. Won't be a problem at all to wait for you."

Bolan nodded and left.

As soon as the Justice man was out of sight, Talbot retrieved the index card from under the report and reached for the phone. Jake Alexander was a political reporter at the *Examiner* who had firsthand information on what went on behind the scenes in Washington. He'd helped Talbot with a murder investigation with a D.C. connection, getting farther into the murky waters of political intrigue than

Talbot had been able to do with his connections through official channels. Alexander was also a friend. He had helped Alexander get off the bottle, and Alexander had helped him get through a divorce.

Raymond came through the squad room doors, popping gum as he leafed through the rap sheet on the girls he'd just booked.

Talbot covered the mouthpiece of the phone as it rang at the other end. "Hey, Alex?"

The young man dropped the papers onto his cluttered desk. "Yeah?"

"Do me a favor and find out what kind of gun was used on Tiep's guys."

"Why?"

"Curiosity."

"Killed the cat, you know." Raymond scooted forward in his chair and stretched for his phone.

"Yeah, well, let's see who else it killed first."

"HAL?"

"Striker, where are you?"

"San Francisco. I'm rattling a few cages down here. You'll probably hear about it soon." Bolan leaned into the pay phone. The Chevy SuperSport was parked at the deserted street corner. He'd checked earlier to make sure Tiep was still sedated and breathing in the trunk. "I need a safehouse to stash a guy in."

"No names?"

"No names. You're already top-heavy with wiring."

"Right."

"And it's going to have to be a place with tight security and guys our side can trust."

Brognola recited an address that the warrior committed to memory, automatically working through the simple code they'd set up to figure out the real address of the safehouse.

"How's it going down there, Striker?"

"It's getting tight. Both IDs are wearing out their welcome. I've been hanging around town too long." Bolan's words were clipped. It hadn't felt good keeping Whit Talbot at arm's length. The detective had seemed like a good cop, ready to help this morning and ready to be suspicious this evening. He was sure Talbot had made the connection between him and Tiep's abduction, and was probably trying to figure an angle to hook it on now; but he didn't want the man to get involved. Taking Gung Quot from his hideout in the building Tiep had named wasn't going to be easy. Or even close to legal.

Quot's team had to be on the move now, he thought, trying to get tonight's delivery arranged and nervous as hell that the violence hadn't ended with Tiep. The biggest card the Executioner had in his deck at the moment was that Quot was no longer a liaison for the CIA first and foremost. The guy was a businessman, and the markets were already getting a little shaky with young DiCarlo's organization thinking of muscling in. Quot couldn't afford to miss the midnight shipment tonight, or some of that market might be easily swayed to the eager Italian competition.

Quot's men would be expecting trouble of some sort, sure, but Bolan was convinced they wouldn't be looking for anything like the hard probe he was planning. Strictly hit-and-git, geared toward popping Quot free of the coverage for a one-on-one that would hopefully net Bolan some intel on the War Memorial assassinations.

If he turned up a dead end, he wasn't sure where he'd try next. Whoever put the lid on the operation in Wonderland had it on tight.

"Striker?"

"Here, Hal. I was just turning things over in my mind."

"Get anything constructive out of it?"

"No."

"I could use some good news."

"Me, too. What's the Man saying about this?"

"I don't know. PR's keeping a shield up around him, broadcasting a lot of shocked outrage. Being onetime chairman of the Department of Dirty Tricks has placed him in a delicate position."

"To say the least."

"Yeah."

"What kind of feel do you have for it, Hal?"

"The same as you do. The Man is clean. Hell, he was nowhere around CIA when this cover-up originated fifteen years ago. We just need to get it cleared away before one of the unfriendly Third World countries starts flinging mud and we can't duck."

Bolan was silent for a moment, then said, "Your department will probably be receiving a call requesting information on me tonight or tomorrow."

"From a certain detective sergeant whose acquaintance you just made?"

"He's already called."

"Bright and early, Striker. He received the standard thanks-but-no-thanks reply. But I had his file pulled in return."

"And?"

"He's a good cop. Tough, loyal, dedicated as hell from what I've been told. And intelligent."

"I gathered that. He's going to be looking for the guy we've got on ice."

"How does he know where to look?"

"Like I said, Hal, both IDs I've been sporting around are beginning to smell. But if everything goes right, I'll be out of here tonight."

"Keep me posted."

Bolan broke the connection and walked back to the Chevy. He'd originally purchased it because it didn't draw attention and allowed him to become part of the background. Fabia and the DiCarlo empire had been shown the fiery red Testarosa that was still parked at the nightclub. All part of the package he was presenting, the role camouflage he'd been relying on for years. Apparently Detective Sergeant Whitman Talbot hadn't bought into the Mike Belasko guise early in the game. Sliding behind the wheel and kicking the big 454 engine to life, Bolan wondered how much trouble that facet of his operation might prove to be.

TALBOT WATCHED the big Justice agent study the schematics with an obviously trained eye. The SFPD detective wrapped his fingers around his coffee cup and pretended to look out at the street all the while studying the warrior's reflection in the window.

Talbot sipped his coffee, finding it cold but refusing to move from his vantage point as he kept surveillance over the Justice agent. He figured he had the scent of the guy, but he wanted something more tangible. Whatever else he proved to be, Belasko wasn't the usual Justice agent. The guy was too much of a pro beneath the easygoing capital cop he pretended to be.

Talbot was also certain Belasko had been behind Tiep's disappearance, but couldn't figure out why the guy was still hanging around or what he hoped to do with the schematics. The bodyguards had been shot with 9 mm parabellums, the same kind of round used by the bastardized Beretta Talbot had glimpsed under Belasko's jacket.

A dark anger boiled inside the detective's large frame. Knowing the man had dropped the bodyguards and coming up with sufficient evidence to interfere in what the Justice Department had sanctioned was worlds apart. In the end Belasko was going to be able to start a virtual gang war between the Vietnamese and the Italians and walk away from it without a care in the world. A lot of people would get killed before the crack trade reestablished stability.

Abruptly Bolan pushed away from Talbot's desk and rolled up the schematics.

"I appreciate the assistance," he said, holding out his hand as Talbot turned to face him.

Talbot took the hand and made an appropriate response, making sure his true feelings didn't show.

"Take care of yourself," Bolan said as he headed for the squad room doors.

"You, too." Was there anything hidden in the big man's words? Talbot wasn't sure. For a moment he wished he'd been able to formulate an unbiased opinion about the man. Professional, true, but what made the guy tick?

As soon as the Warrior disappeared from sight, Talbot returned to his desk and pulled open a drawer. He shrugged into his shoulder holster, buckled the big .45 into the rig instead of the customary S&W long-barreled .38, clipped a .38 Special to his belt over his right hip and tucked a 4-shot .357 COP into an ankle holster. Then, snaring his charcoal-colored suit jacket from the back of his chair, he slipped into it, making sure it covered the hardware. Looking at Raymond, who was watching with a bemused expression, frozen in midchew, he said, "If Mandy calls, tell her I'll see her in a little while."

Raymond nodded mechanically. "Where are you going?"

Stamping his right leg to make sure the ankle holster was secure, Talbot said, "To get a breath of fresh air."

"You figure somebody's going to try to take it away from you?"

Talbot let a thin smile twist his lips as he wrote the address of the building on the schematics on an index card. "You never know, Alex. This is a tough city." He added a box of ammo for the .45 as an afterthought.

BOLAN PARKED the Chevy three blocks from the address in a dank, littered alley. He stripped off the civilian clothes quickly, feeling the skin-tightening embrace of the night air, then donned the blacksuit. Combat cosmetics darkened his face and hands.

The military webbing went on next, with the Beretta 93-R riding in its accustomed place under his left arm while the Desert Eagle .44 rode his right hip. He rammed a magazine into an Uzi and slung it across his back. A Franchi SPAS 12 with a foldout stock rested comfortably from its nylon belt around his right shoulder. Finally the warrior retrieved an oversize black trench coat from the back seat.

Gear in place and checked, coat concealing his armament, the Executioner moved out to define the perimeters for tonight's hellzone.

3

Bolan watched the delivery van roll to a stop outside the target building at 11:47, thirteen minutes ahead of schedule. The Executioner had made his way to the roof of the building over an hour ago when he finished his recon, slipping easily through the cordon Gung Quot's men had tried to establish.

The streets in the area were deserted at this time of night. Maybe on Fridays or Saturdays they would show a little life, but Bolan didn't figure it would be much. Which had to be one of Quot's reasons for handling the transaction at this time on a Tuesday night.

One man got out of the van and rolled back a metal door, and Bolan shifted as the red brake lights of the van disappeared inside the building, checking the guard's positions with the small infrared binoculars he held. So far, so good.

The men Quot had stationed around the perimeter would be good, but they were jaded from living a life of luxury. Quot's organization had too many cops on the take and the deal with the old DiCarlo regime had been too sweet. Even Tiep's disappearance hadn't been enough to jolt them out of the rut of carelessness they'd fallen into.

Numbers began filing through the warrior's head, counting down to the opening round of his planned strike.

He stood and shrugged out of the trench coat, throwing a leg over the building's edge as he gripped the thin nylon cord connected to the grappling hook he'd placed earlier. His hands tensed under the leather gloves as they took his body weight, beginning the three-story descent. He didn't use his legs to take any of the drag off his arms as he let the cord move through the gloves in a controlled slide, melding his body to the building's protective shadow. His palms heated up inside the gloves from the friction; his shoulders ached from the extra weight of the gear.

Perspiration caused by the exertion beaded his forehead as he dropped the last few feet to a soundless landing. Approximately forty-five seconds had passed since he'd reached the alley. Now that the cast was in place, he could kick the opening numbers into play.

Bolan retrieved an electronic detonator from a pocket of the blacksuit and edged around the corner of the building, keeping the positions of Quot's men clearly marked in his mind. He activated the device and clipped it to his shoulder harness beside the 93-R, then slipped the safety off the SPAS.

The shotgun felt like a lean, hard bar in his hands, but he was more than familiar with the sheer knockdown power afforded by the grim-looking weapon, which was why he'd chosen the SPAS for his lead weapon in this hit-and-git strike. There was no telling how many of Quot's men used crack themselves. The lighter 9 mm loads of the Beretta and Uzi might not be enough to knock the guards down and keep them down if he was forced to take them out.

He kept his back to the brick exterior of the building as he edged toward the sheet metal doors through which the delivery van had just vanished.

A dim shadow separated itself from the building across the street. Bolan froze, marking the movement with the barrel of the SPAS, ready to bring the shotgun into target acquisition at the first sign of a threat from that quarter.

The shadow faded back into the blurred outlines of the building. A heartbeat later the warm orange glow of a cigarette burned a hole in the darkness.

Glancing at the recessed area of the sheet metal doors, Bolan saw a boot sticking out from the man posted there. He slipped his finger out of the trigger guard as he edged closer, freeing the stock of the SPAS from his hip. Then the Executioner twisted around the recessed area quickly, hefting the heavy shotgun to smash into the guard's face before the man could react.

A dull pop sounded when the SPAS connected with the guard's forehead, followed immediately by a muted thud as the man slammed into the brick wall behind him. Bolan caught the unconscious guard one-handed, using the loose folds of the guy's jacket to settle him on the sidewalk gently without making any noise. Moving into the guard's vacated position, Bolan glanced through the wire-meshed window framed in the upper half of the side entrance. He knew he was outlined against the uncertain light out on the street, but also knew that he wouldn't be recognized.

A low-wattage bulb hung from the high concrete ceiling, throwing a dusting of illumination over the two vehicles inside. The delivery van was closer to Bolan, obscuring the last third of the steel-gray Lincoln Continental that had arrived first. Judging from the way the town car sat on the steel-belted radials, Quot had financed some heavy reconstruction on the vehicle, starting with bulletproof glass and body armor.

Bolan had been counting on that.

Three men were bathed in the weak yellow light of the naked bulb, concluding business. Bolan recognized Gung Quot from the description McFee had provided; the triangular burn scar on the man's right cheek made it official.

Quot barely hit the five-foot-six mark and was reed-thin. Still, the Vietnamese maintained a presence around him that was palpable. His hair, though absent on top, fell to his shoulders in the back, offset by the long goatee dripping from his chin. His clothes were expensive, making him a match for the car in fashion if not in demeanor. Yet, like the heaviness of the Lincoln indicated by the bulging tires, Quot exuded an air of having more depth than was immediately apparent.

The two other men were from the delivery van, and their coveralls displayed the logo of the delivery service on the back. The Uzi in each man's possession dangled from a shoulder strap as they stood in front of the open bay of the van.

Quot's voice didn't carry past the closed entrance, but judging from his stance and the way he kept speaking in a clipped fashion, Bolan guessed the man was asking questions concerning Tiep's whereabouts. The conversation ended abruptly, and Quot turned to slide back into the rear of the Lincoln, much to the two deliverymen's evident relief.

Bolan dropped back into the shadows as the Lincoln's headlights flared to life. Smoky gray vapor trailed thinly from the vehicle's undercarriage. Nudging the protective cover from the electronic detonator, the Executioner poised a finger over the button and waited.

The building was old, built only a short time after the earthquake of 1906 that destroyed twenty-eight thousand buildings and swallowed the infamous Barbary Coast. The foundation of the building, like the ceiling of the parking area, had been formed from thick concrete slabs. According to the information Talbot's connection had been able to turn up, the building had been deserted since a private detective agency specializing in repos had vacated the premises eight years earlier. The name of the business that now owned the building didn't match up with any of the intel Bolan had been able to put together on Quot's organization, but he was sure it tracked back to the crack supplier. Bolan assumed the parking area had been for the repossessed cars the detective agency secured, because the last building permit issued at the site had been fourteen years ago when the agency set up shop. Gray grease spots still dotted the dingy concrete floor with only a few new places showing.

Bolan flashed the specs of the floor through his head once more and the numbers dropped to zero. The rickety wooden stairway leading to the second-floor office area filled with musty, stained carpets had held his weight when he'd gone up before Quot's men arrived, even though some of the planks had complained in squeaks. There was no other access to the second floor.

The steel-gray continental rolled forward as a garage door opener operated by the driver started the sheet metal doors to open. Bolan hit the detonator and felt the immediate *whump* of explosives shiver through the brick wall behind him. Concrete dust and rolling thunder belched out into the street as the metal doors tried to find a variety of new positions. Folded double and frayed at the corners, they slumped to a final rest in the center of the garage opening.

Bolan ripped the entrance door open and lunged inside, the SPAS up and ready, aware that startled shadows had peeled from the buildings across the street and were double-timing it toward him. One of the Uzi-wielding deliverymen stepped from the open bay of the van, bringing the snout of his weapon to waist level as his eyes locked on the Executioner. A blast of high-brass double-aught buckshot from the SPAS shredded the man's chest and slammed him back into the van.

Still on the move, the numbers relentlessly pushing him on, Bolan triggered another round from the shotgun, dissolving the front windshield of the van. The Lincoln had come to an abrupt stop only a few feet from the garage entrance. Whole sections of the concrete ceiling had been blown apart by the charges Bolan had placed earlier, leaving dark, gaping holes in the second-level floor. Falling concrete had dented the town car and smashed the front window into a mesh of fine-veined cracks. The driver tried to force the door open, creating a screech of metal on metal that drew Bolan's instant attention. Knowing it wouldn't penetrate the bulletproof glass, the Executioner splintered the polarized window of the driver's door with a charge from the SPAS, changing the guy's mind about leaving the vehicle.

A flicker of movement near the shattered garage door caught Bolan's eye. Reaching into a pocket of the blacksuit, he retrieved a grenade and flipped it toward the opening. He heard a man yell a warning that was cut off halfway by the exploding grenade.

The warrior fed more shells into the shotgun, then drew the Desert Eagle, keeping a low profile against the van. An Uzi poked around the shattered garage entrance, followed by a head. The booming report of the .44 shivered through the parking area and the head disappeared, yanking the corpse out into the street.

Bullets ripped through the thin metal of the van as the hidden deliveryman targeted in on the sound of Bolan's

Desert Eagle. The ruptures formed a ragged Z as the automatic weapon cycled dry. Pushing up from the prone position he'd adopted, Bolan leathered the big .44 as he ducked into the bay door of the van. The gunner had just finished reloading when the Executioner spotted him. Bolan squeezed the trigger of the SPAS, bracing the stock against his hip. The shotgun recoiled painfully into his pelvic bone with enough force to leave bruises, but the charge punched the gunner through the rear of the van, the corpse sprawling onto the concrete floor.

A hail of lead sprayed into the interior of the van, gouging the walls as the outside guards searched for Bolan. The warrior leaped free of the vehicle and threw himself forward, skidding on his elbows as he brought the 12-gauge to his shoulder. Apparently he'd missed a pair of roving sentries during the outside head count, a potentially fatal error in a killzone. He was dimly aware of the Lincoln's driver kicking the ignition over and heard the big engine catch. His first shot from the SPAS took out the guard to his left and he readjusted his aim, bringing the other man into target acquisition.

The Lincoln's tires squealed on the concrete as they fought to break free of the rubble holding the vehicle, the power steering belt whining as the driver explored the extent of the maneuverability left to him. Chips flew like razor-sharp daggers as the shooter standing behind the collapsed bulk of the sheet metal doors brought the line of fire closer, leaving hollowed-out pockmarks on the concrete floor. The SPAS thudded into Bolan's shoulder, and a load of buckshot clawed through the sheet metal and ripped the shooter almost in two just as the whining tires of the Lincoln found purchase and shuddered the big car free straight at Bolan.

Reacting instantly, the Executioner rolled out of the way. The big car slammed into the wall beside the warrior, breaking holes in the concrete blocks and crumpling the fender.

Trusting the armor plating to protect the car's occupants, Bolan tossed a grenade under the Lincoln as he took refuge behind the shattered van. The explosion was deafening, and for a moment it seemed as though someone had fired lightning into the building. Blinking against the flickering afterimages, Bolan regained his footing and raced for the car.

The blast had lifted the Lincoln from the floor and dropped it back onto the rubble, canting it to one side. Bolan knew that Quot and the driver had to be badly shaken by the blast, but didn't now how quickly they'd be able to shake off the effects.

The warrior dropped the SPAS, drew the Desert Eagle and yanked the rear door open. The sharp scent of gasoline was strong, and something was smoking under the hood of the big luxury car.

The door gave grudgingly, and the driver moved more quickly than the Executioner would have thought possible, fumbling with a big automatic. Triggering a round, Bolan punched a 240-grain hollowpoint between the driver's eyes. The man's body dropped from sight with the force of the impact.

Quot tried to fight back as Bolan grabbed him roughly by his jacket and hauled him out of the Continental. Blood flowed from a wound in the Vietnamese's forehead. He reached for the gun he'd dropped on the car seat, but Bolan slammed the guy against the car, then whirled Quot around to face him.

"Who the hell are you?" Quot asked in Vietnamese. His eyes had trouble focusing. He put a hand to his forehead and brushed blood away, smearing it along his fingers.

Something spattered under Bolan's boot, and he looked down to find gasoline swirling greasy rainbows around their feet. The smell of smoke was stronger now, and curling black wisps rose from the car.

Bolan realized that some of Quot's men were still active. He knotted a hand in the crack dealer's tie and pulled him along as he moved toward the rickety stairway on the other side of the car. How much longer would it be before the police were on the scene? Couldn't be more than a few minutes at most. Frankly he was surprised they weren't already there at Talbot's request.

A volley of shots cut new holes in the Lincoln's bodywork. Bringing up the Desert Eagle in a two-handed grip, Bolan directed three rounds into the mass of twisted sheet metal blocking the garage opening, knowing the basso booming of the hollowpoints striking the metal would dampen some of his attacker's enthusiasm.

"Mad Dog?" Quot asked as he stumbled up the stairs. "Are you with Mad Dog?"

Bolan tried to make some sense of the name as he followed the man up the steps. Mad Dog sounded like a code name, but for what? And why did Quot sound as if he were expecting somebody?

Quot halted in the center of the stairway, facing Bolan with a panic-stricken gaze. "How much are they paying you?" he demanded.

"I don't know what you're talking about."

"You aren't a cop," Quot said. He tried to grin, but the effort didn't pay off. "A cop wouldn't be alone in an operation like this, let alone try to pull it off in the first place."

Bolan took a moment to sort it out, remembering the way Tiep had been afraid of him, too, and hadn't been surprised about someone from the Agency looking for Quot. Quot was expecting him. Or expecting someone. Either way Bolan figured he'd hit pay dirt. If he lived long enough to mine the vein.

Someone hurtled headlong over the pile of rubble, dodging for cover behind the smashed Continental. Bolan placed a hand on Quot's shoulder and turned him around, then shoved the man ahead of him up the stairs.

Bullets from the hidden gunner's weapon gouged chunks of wood from the stairway, shaking the structure with tremors. Bolan sprinted up the steps, feeling one of them give way beneath him with a sickening wrench. Flailing his arms, he caught the railing with his free hand and stopped his fall. He sent two rounds skipping over the hood of the Lincoln, driving the gunner to cover as he recovered his footing.

Flames darted out from under the Continental with a soft whoosh, spreading a blue-and-yellow-tongued torch that scurried across the surface of the gasoline draining from the cracked tank.

Quot had vanished into the scarcely broken darkness of the upper floor. Bolan had almost made it when the car exploded and tore the wooden stairway out from under him in a vicious crack-the-whip.

SERGEANT WHIT TALBOT HAD almost exhausted his vast store of patience before he heard the first explosion. He'd seen the steel-gray Lincoln continental and the delivery van enter the building ten minutes ago, but he hadn't seen Belasko. For an hour and a half he'd sat in his unmarked car torturing himself with the remembered flavor of cigarettes. But stakeouts like the one he was currently engaged in was the chief reason he'd quit smoking. A man couldn't very well sit in a car at night watching somebody while he torched a cigarette.

The Department of Motor Vehicles had let him know the Continental belonged to somebody named Henry Po, who had a clean record and an address up on Telegraph Hill near Coit Tower. His cop's instinct wanted him to push for exploration, maybe give his chief a call and see about getting a warrant to search the building, except he knew from experience what kind of invective the chief was partial to using at this time of night. Especially when a homicide cop started sticking his nose into vice business, and maybe even business belonging to the Department of Justice at that. And if it was a drug deal the way he thought it was, the transaction would be completed before he could even get the uniforms in the area. If worst came to worst, he could try to tail the Continental and see about arranging a bust in transit. Mahoney was still trying to make the detective grade and wouldn't mind pulling a car over for a "faulty" taillight.

Talbot was also thinking he'd need more information on what exactly was going on before pursuing Belasko any farther. Maybe the schematics had been part of something the Justice man was still moving on and wouldn't be needing for a few more days yet. Maybe something else had developed and refocused the case the big man was working on. Or maybe, Talbot thought sourly, the whole schematic angle was just a scam to throw him off the trail. Belasko had known he was curious and suspicious of the Tiep snatch. Talbot thought it was just the kind of thing he himself would have pulled to stop somebody from looking over his shoulder while he tried to do his job.

Then the front of the building he'd been watching exploded and guys were running for the mangled garage door. He automatically reached for the car radio.

He made the call, turning in his unit number, his location and the explosive nature of the squeal. Then he was out of the car, trotting down the street with both hands wrapped around the .45, wishing to hell he'd taken the time to talk to Mandy. You never knew when your number would come up.

Another explosion jarred the street, throwing one of the guys backward from the garage. Talbot could hear automatic fire coming from inside the building now, punctuated by roaring shotgun blasts.

One of the men firing into the building caught sight of him and whirled around, bringing up an Uzi. Talbot threw himself into the gutter, maintaining his two-handed grip on the automatic as he fell. A short burst passed harmlessly over his head. Holding the .45 centered on the man's chest, Talbot snapped off three rounds, knowing the last one probably missed but not hesitating just the same.

The man crumpled to the ground.

"Police!" Talbot yelled as he hauled himself to his feet. He couldn't tell if the three men in front of him could hear him over another ear-rupturing explosion. One guy bolted, disappearing inside the building.

Grabbing the cover offered by the corner of the building, Talbot placed his back to the bricks and held the .45 at chin level. He took a quick glance around the corner, lined up the automatic on the nearer man and yelled, "Drop the goddamn gun now!"

The man spun, raking a vicious spray of autofire that wreaked havoc against the wall. Talbot dropped the hammer in a controlled squeeze, breathing out slowly as if he were on the range shooting for six-packs. The guy clutched his abdomen, and the Uzi clattered to the sidewalk.

Talbot caught a glimpse of the other man, cutting out for the building. Holding the .45 in both hands, the detective advanced on the bodies strewn in front of the building. Gunfire still crackled inside the parking area, and he could see smoke filtering from inside to stain the night air.

He rolled over the first man that he came to, finding no face to make a possible ID. The next one was the first shooter he'd capped. He recognized him immediately from the Tiep file he'd gotten for Belasko that morning. Score a big one for the homicide detective, he thought. Now if he didn't get his butt shot off in this firefight by one side or the other, he'd be goddamn lucky.

Screeching tires drew Talbot's attention from the third corpse. The late-model sedan came to a rocky and uneven stop less than twenty feet from his position. He made out two guys in the front seat, one of whom held a semiautomatic rifle. He kept the .45 aimed at the guy, aware of the fact that he had no cover to retreat to. Where the hell was the backup?

The guy with the rifle stepped out of the car with an easy smile. He was young, and dressed in a three-piece suit. Talbot felt better at once. None of the bodies around him were wearing three-piece suits.

"If you're not a cop," the guy said, "then I just made a big mistake."

"No mistake," Talbot replied as he dropped the .45. "Name's Talbot. I'm with Homicide."

"Looks like you're about ankle deep in your work tonight, Sergeant."

Alarm bells went off in Talbot's head. He hadn't mentioned his rank, which meant these guys knew him. But how? Belasko? He doubted it. The big Justice man had been a loner. Talbot had sensed that right off. And why would Belasko's buddies just now be getting into the act?

As if realizing he'd made a mistake, the guy with the rifle brought his weapon up and fired several shots at point-blank range. Talbot staggered backward and collapsed onto one of the corpses. He felt blood running down the inside of his left arm and couldn't feel his chest at all. He tried to breathe and couldn't. Tires squealed as the sedan moved out, its lights shooting across the detective's legs. He struggled to move, but nothing worked. Only the emptiness in his chest seemed alive.

The thought that Belasko's troubles inside the building had just gotten worse drifted fuzzily across his mind, then everything went black.

4

The soft buzzing of the alarm system tripped a handful of seconds after former Army Major Shane Innis became aware someone had boarded his yacht. He tapped the security panel, turning off the faintly audible beeping.

Moving cautiously, Innis switched the security system off, noticing the lambent emerald lights fade to nothing in the periphery of his vision. He sat up in bed, a big hand already cupping the Colt Delta Elite 10 mm he kept under his pillow. Listening, he breathed deeply, keeping his heart rate down to a level that didn't interfere with his hearing.

He stepped out of bed, naked, then reached for the two extra clips to the Colt that were also under the pillow. He didn't bother slipping the safety off. When he went to sleep at night, he never put it on.

The hair on the back of Innis's neck bristled in an animal awareness, deeply ingrained from thirty years of war in at least half as many countries. He crouched, moving carefully now as he made his way to the nearest window. A slight breeze swept in from the upper deck, bringing with it a brief coolness and the lingering after-scent of brine, sweat and hydraulic fluid. The yacht rocked slowly beneath his feet, riding out the gentle ocean swells. But it was a motion he was accustomed to. The sounds were familiar, too, except for one—the hesitant sloshing against the upper deck.

Innis glanced out the window, staring out over the wrinkled placidness of the Atlantic Ocean that separated his yacht and the pier from the line of modern buildings spreading across Luanda.

He tightened his grip on the Colt.

"Hurry up!" a man whispered in a Bantu dialect that Innis had become familiar with during the past thirteen years.

Angola had become home to Innis after the Vietnam War, and he'd been forced to learn Portuguese as well as a smattering of a handful of Bantu dialects. Learning enough to converse about money and war was easy no matter what the language, and a jungle was still a jungle. His soldiering in South Africa had been no different from what he'd done in Vietnam, with a few territorial variations. He'd just been paid better.

In response to the whispered command, the sloshing on the deck increased.

So there were at least two guys, Innis concluded as he moved away from the window. But who did they belong to? He and his merc team had worked for a lot of people since the end of the war. They'd had to in order to stay alive. Uncle Sammy had wanted Innis and his former unit dead even more than the North Vietnamese. The Hawks, better known then as Satan's Backup, were supposed to be the last American casualties of the Vietnam War, with full benefits paid to their survivors and a hero's burial, a twenty-one-gun salute and the whole nine yards. Operation Mad Dog, the CIA had called their planned demise in 1975. It could have been successful, too, if Drew Judson, their control, hadn't confirmed Innis's suspicions about the coming assassination attempt. Instead of being the victims, Innis had led his team to a bloody victory against superior forces marshaled by CIA agents he'd previously worked for.

But Innis had played it safe even after that. According to CIA files, Major Shane Innis had perished with his Special Forces team a few days later when their plane was shot down over Cambodia. Innis had even been considerate enough to leave the required number of bodies to cover a head count the Agency made later to confirm their deaths.

So the guys dousing the yacht probably didn't have anything to do with the Agency, but Innis didn't rule it out altogether. Judson had said there were still periodic checks on him conducted by the CIA station chiefs who were in Vietnam and had been connected with Operation Mad Dog. Innis could remember a meeting with his former control about nine years ago when Judson said the spooks probably wouldn't be completely satisfied about Innis's alleged death until they actually saw him in the grave. With a stake through his heart.

Innis grinned at the memory.

Yeah. That was what had inspired Mad Dog: that same kind of fear. Even the Agency hardasses had been afraid of the Hawks. And Innis. The CIA had selected most of the team's work early in the war, throwaway missions that had sometimes seemed to be sheer suicide going in. But the Hawks had survived and come waltzing back to base—mission accomplished—a few days later. The problem was, not all of those missions had been squeaky clean, nor would they have been looked on in favor by the American people.

Only three people knew he owned the yacht, and they knew only the alias under which he and his merc team operated. Most of the fishermen who worked these waters thought he was a Briton with varied business interests that took him over most of South Africa. Others thought he was a Soviet spy or had defected from the KGB.

Lately a lot of his mercenary work had been in Namibia, with Angola's blessing, as he helped the South-West African People's Organization sort out their difficulties in becoming independent. Namibia paid well, but the powers that be were battling against the combined but separate interests of South Africa and the United Nations.

It was possible, Innis told himself as he reached quietly back into a hallway closet for a pair of pants and a lightweight sweater, that the men dumping gasoline on the deck were connected with the South Africans. The team's profile hadn't been low lately, and they had been followed back to a base camp after making a recent strike in Windhoek. He dressed himself and tucked a pair of tennis shoes in the back pockets of the jeans.

Less than two minutes had passed since he first heard the noise that had awakened him.

"Let's go!" the whispered voice urged. "You've got enough on there!"

Liquid splashed on the port side of the yacht and bare feet slapped against the deck above Innis's head. Innis moved forward, coming to a crouch just inside the doorway of the cabin. A dark shadow crossed his field of vision on the starboard side.

Standing abruptly, he steadied the Colt 10 mm on the combing beside the cabin and unloaded two rounds into the back of the man who was trying to scramble from the aft starboard side of the yacht. His victim screamed in an ululating wail that crackled across the pierfront and ended in an abrupt choking just before a heavy splash.

"Damn it!" someone shouted. "Get the bastard before he escapes!"

"There he is!"

Innis threw himself over the side, angling his fall into a dive that would give him considerable depth. Before he cleaved the water he heard the sound of shattering glass and the whoosh of what he took to be a wall of flame. Then the water closed over Innis's head, muffling most of the noise.

One of the assassins shone a flashlight in his direction, forming an ever-widening column of pale light that failed to penetrate the umber depths of the Atlantic. Innis let himself sink into the ocean, moving only enough to shove the Colt into the waistband of his pants.

More circles of flashlights had joined the first, skidding frantically across the placid ocean surface. Then bullets ripped through the water, leaving streamers of green and white twisting in their backwash, never coming close to Innis's position.

Satisfied that the men couldn't see him, Innis stroked for the other side of the yacht. He passed under the dark bulk, swimming on his back, pulling himself along hand over hand on the slime-slick surface. Lungs near the bursting point, he glimpsed more bullets searching the still waters, this time joined by fiery green tracer rounds. He decided he could stay under a little longer.

When black spots became visible against the darkness of the ocean, Innis swam to the concrete pier and inched his way up until his face was out of the water. He took long, shuddering breaths, sucking them in as quietly as he could, blinking his eyes against the stinging brine.

Where were they?

He could hear them shouting to one another now, and cursing at the curious fishermen who were starting to gather. Small vibrations of the running feet tingled his hands pressed palm first against the concrete pier. The fire on the yacht had spread quickly, arcing up into the night sky with questing fingers of flame at least twenty feet high.

Pushing off from the pier, Innis swam south, away from Luanda. He felt the immediate threat dying away with every stroke, feeling the hot coals of anger moving in to take its place. The yacht fireballed without warning, sending a roiling orange- and black-flamed mushroom rushing skyward.

He paused to watch the fire die down. Several of the fishermen were on the pier now, rushing to save their boats. Wild screams of panic and rage filled the air. The yacht meant little to Innis, less than the fishing boats did to the fishermen, certainly. It had been a place to regroup between wars or recover from injuries.

He pulled himself out of the water a hundred yards from the burning wreckage and slipped on the tennis shoes as he scanned the crowded pier for the men who had tried to kill him. The rage locked inside him had reached a fever pitch that beat steadily in his temples.

One hand clutching the Colt under the heavy folds of the dripping sweater, Innis worked his way back toward the yacht, the crowd making way for him as he strode down the concrete pier. He raked wet hair from his eyes and smoothed it into the slicked-back style he favored. Catching sight of a white man with an AK-47 cradled in his arms, Innis stepped onto the nearest fishing boat and helped the old man and two young boys sort through the tangled lines and hawsers as they struggled to get the fishing boat out into safer waters. His hand never left the automatic.

Innis kept his back to the armed man, watching his attacker pass by without seeing him, intent on watching the sea beyond the fishing boats. One lithe leap put him behind the man, the Colt pressing into his spinal cord. The man froze.

"Do you speak English, asshole?" Innis grated in his ear. When the response was slow in coming, he prodded the man with the pistol.

"Yes."

"Good." Innis glanced over his shoulder to see if anyone had taken notice. Then he looked back at his prisoner. "How many of you are there?"

The Russian assault rifle quivered in the man's hands.

"Try it, junior, and you're dead."

"Six."

"Better, much better. Move over to the side of the pier. Do I need to tell you to do it slowly?"

The man shook his head.

"Move."

He could smell fear on the man in front of him, mixed in with the fish and diesel odors, but unmistakable just the same. They came to a halt at the edge of the pier. "Drop the AK."

Holding the rifle by the barrel, the man let it slide through his fingers. Against the background of misfiring engines and hoarse shouts for help, it made no noise at all when it hit the water.

Innis prodded the man with the Colt's barrel. "Remember what I've got in my hand, cowboy, and don't try anything."

The man nodded.

Pulling the 10 mm out of his prisoner's back, Innis asked, "Who are you with?"

"Wait! We can cut a deal!"

Amused, Innis asked, "What kind of deal?"

The man's voice held a desperate edge of hysteria. "I can tell them I found your body, Innis. They'll think you're dead."

"Hacker didn't think I was dead last time."

The man closed his eyes and trembled.

Innis prodded him with the automatic. "How did Hacker know where to find me?"

"Lawrence had some stuff that led Hacker to believe you were here in Angola."

"Where's Lawrence?"

"He's dead."

"Hacker?"

"No."

"Who?"

"We don't know. Somebody took him out and left a note with his name on it. Then marked through his name on the Vietnam War Memorial in Washington."

"When?"

"A couple of weeks ago."

"It took you two weeks to find me?"

"You're not an easy man to find, Innis, and Hacker wants to keep this whole thing under the carpet."

"I bet he does."

More and more of the fishing boats were pulling away from the pier. Innis knew it would be only a few more minutes before the area was deserted, giving his hunters a clear shot at him.

"So what about the deal?"

Innis tucked the automatic into his waistband. "Sure."

The man breathed a sigh of relief and started to turn around. The weak grin on the guy's face became a grimace of terror as Innis grabbed his head in both hands and twisted violently. Vertebrae cracked. The man's body went slack, and with a shove from Innis, tumbled into the dark water.

He paused to watch it sink. "A deal is a deal, guy. When I see Hacker, I'll tell him you're dead."

On the heels of the outward-bound fishermen, Innis eased himself away from the pier and away from the hunters.

Hacker. The name brought burning memories of a need for retribution. It had been Hacker who had issued Operation Mad Dog.

Once out of the immediate vicinity of the pier, Innis broke into a jog. He palmed the automatic as much as he could, hiding the rest of it under his wrist and forearm.

Who had killed Lawrence? Innis wondered as he ran. He could believe Hacker had guessed his home base from stuff Lawrence kept. Lawrence was a natural packrat. The man had been a damn good point in an operation, but Lawrence would take anything that wasn't tied down.

If Hacker had killed Lawrence, the agent Innis had killed wouldn't have denied it. Even if Lawrence had been accidently killed, the identity Judson had helped build up over the years would have covered any ties with the Hawks. But the CIA guy had said that whoever had taken out Lawrence had crossed his former friend's name off the Vietnam War Memorial. Why?

A challenge?

But from who? And why?

Only Hacker and two other guys in the United States would have had any reason to be hunting him or the other Hawks. And after fifteen years, Innis had thought most of the searching would have been over.

Evidently, for someone, it was only beginning.

Innis grinned as he jogged, reveling in the exertion. You were only as young as you felt, he told himself. And with an unknown hunter on his tail, he felt like a kid again, getting intimate with the jungle for the first time. Except he couldn't erase his experience, or the confidence. He relished the thought of the unknown hunter's blood on his hands just as he was saddened by the inevitability of it. It felt good to have to be thinking on the run again, wondering how much the enemy knew about you, trying to guess how much of a head start you had and could maintain.

Innis hoped the hunter could stay out of Hacker's reach long enough for him to get back stateside.

REELING SLIGHTLY as the shock of the leg wound set in, Khoi hobbled down the short incline to the South Canadian River. The sand, a thick carpet under his feet, soaked up his blood as well as Mitch Henderson's.

Henderson—Corporal Mike Drake during the war—was farther up the hill, his body concealed at the moment by the trees he had tried to hide in.

The man had been so quick, Khoi thought as he lifted his injured leg over the barbed wire fence running parallel with the river. He tore his black sweatpants up the inside until he reached the wound, then sat down, drawing in controlled breaths, relaxing the tense muscles, willing the pain to fade away.

The bullet had left a blue-black hole through the fleshy part of his left thigh that still oozed scarlet. Slipping the tight-fitting black gloves from his hands, Khoi inspected the wound. It would be more painful than dangerous, he realized, then shivered slightly when he noticed how close Henderson's bullet had come to emasculating him.

Then he grimaced at his own thoughts. He had no right to think of the future. Thinking of the future took his attention from his chosen task at hand.

He felt the back of his leg, finding the numbed and slippery hole of the exit wound, sickened yet grateful that the bullet had passed through.

And where would he make this glorious future his thoughts had placed in his mind? Back in Vietnam? Here in the United States? Neither place held anything for him, yet both had contributed to his birth.

There was no future, he told himself as he took his headband off to use as a bandage. There was no future.

Because there had been no past.

Because of the actions of the men he tracked, Khoi had lived as an outcast in his uncle's village, suffered only because his mother had been willing to fight for him. No matter what else Khoi was, she had said, he was still of her flesh. Still her son.

Hot tears rushed down the young man's face as he remembered. His mother had protected him, yes, but she had died when he was fourteen. He'd spent the next ten years living with the Meo tribesmen, but he'd never become close to any of them. Many had tried to know him, but he was unable to respond to their efforts. He was tainted. How many times had he heard his uncle say that? And his mother would scream and curse at her brother, then cry so quietly when she thought she was alone.

Some of the feeling was returning to the young man's leg now, bringing pain with it. Khoi wiped his face, seeing Henderson's blood come away on his fingers. He'd been very close to the man when he killed him. He would have to burn his clothes.

He rolled over on his stomach and brushed away the surface scum of the slow-moving river. The water was tepid and had a dirty taste, but it alleviated the dryness at the back of his throat.

The night came alive around him again after being startled into silence by the sound of the shots. A frog jumped into the water somewhere nearby; a bird he couldn't identify let out a mournful wail that echoed pure loneliness; the insects clacked, scratched and whistled, and flickered briefly against the darkness.

Khoi took another drink, then stood, bringing up the comfortable weight of the Uzi with him. A Ka-bar was suspended upside down from the military webbing across his shoulders, and he used it to cut the pant leg off at the knee so that it wouldn't keep catching in the tall grass growing among the trees farther up the incline. He'd left the Jeep about a mile away, near Henderson's vehicle. The walk back would be arduous, but at least he didn't have to hurry or worry about being apprehended. The Oklahoma town Henderson had lived in for the past twelve years didn't have a regular police force. Khoi had discovered that during his investigation of the man yesterday.

Henderson had been the easiest to find of the three men he had executed so far. But the smallness of the town had also worked against Khoi. Henderson had led him here tonight, and had been waiting in the darkness, already aware someone was after him.

The only thing that had saved the young Vietnamese was the man's curiosity about who Khoi was and who he represented. Even then, Henderson's speed and agility almost kept him alive.

Three of the men were dead. Khoi didn't know where the rest of them were, which was why he had let them know he was coming for them. They would be moving now, he realized, making mistakes and leaving a trail for him to follow. It had taken him over a year of searching in the United States to find even the first one. But Judson had been their liaison with the CIA and had protected them when the order for their deaths had been issued. The big American who had married into the Meos after the war, Smiley, had told him that. Smiley had been concerned about Khoi's decision to join Gung Quot's Vietnam cocaine outlet and had tried to dissuade the young man from getting involved with the men. But the information, gleaned from Smiley during several talks, only reinforced Khoi's decision to join.

He reached under the dead man's arms and dragged him down the incline so that his body would be found more quickly. Kneeling, he took the piece of paper containing his victim's real name from a pocket of his shirt and pinned it to the dead man. He wouldn't have to cross out this man's name on the Vietnam War Memorial in Washington. The news media had been filled with the stories of his first two executions. The name would be enough. And the others would know he was coming.

Khoi pushed himself erect, wishing he could feel even a fraction of the satisfaction he thought he would experience by tracking these men down. Even if they hadn't brutalized his mother, to him, these men deserved to die. Smiley had told him they were killers, evil men, running through the jungles of Vietnam partaking not of war but of slaughter. Innocents had gone down under their guns, women and children. They had left Khoi's mother for dead in the same village they had burned to the ground. And one of them had cut her ear off. As a trophy. Smiley had told Khoi the men did that, too.

Vengeance.

Maybe it wouldn't be as satisfying as he thought, but Khoi refused to give it up. It had been the only thing in his life for many years. And it wasn't just vengeance for his mother and himself. It was for the others, too—the ones he had talked with as he searched for traces of these men in Vietnam; the ones who had been left without mothers, fathers, children, without peace at night, fearing those men would stalk the jungles again.

Taking up a fistful of sand from the riverbank, he let it trickle through his fingers onto the dead man's chest. Then he began the long walk back to the Jeep.

5

Fingertips of one hand barely clinging to the doorsill to the second floor, Bolan dangled for a moment as the wooden stairway collapsed beneath him. Leathering the .44, he reached over his head and secured a better hold on the flooring, aware that Quot might be waiting in the darkness above him. He got an elbow over the threshold and pulled himself up.

The orange glare of the gasoline fire poured serrated shadows into the narrow hallway.

Where was Quot?

Bolan peered into the wavering blackness as he drew the Desert Eagle. Scrapes along his elbows were aching after the mad scramble onto the floor. He ignored the minor pain as he moved quietly down the hallway.

Somebody tripped in the darkness ahead of him. Bolan moved toward the sound, holding the .44 at the ready, aware that yellow tongues from the fire below were already lapping at the walls. His night vision kicked in as he left the area.

The warrior jogged down the hallway until he found what appeared to be the main office, which overlooked the front of the building. He spotted Quot, just as the man was getting to his feet. He reached for the Vietnamese, then jerked his arm back when he saw something glimmer in the man's hand. Holding his ground, Bolan raised the .44 to a point that occupied all of Quot's attention.

For a moment both men froze. Bolan could feel the slight breeze coming in through the broken window to their left, heard the sudden screech of tires on the street below, could taste the old mustiness and new smoke that was filtering into the room. But he saw nothing except the short four-inch knife clasped in Quot's hand.

The cut on Quot's forehead still bled and had turned half of his face into a bloody mask. "Kill me," he said. "They sent you here to do that. Do it."

"I'm not here to kill you," Bolan replied. "All I want to do is talk."

"About what?"

"About who killed Lawrence and Stoddard after they were reported dead fifteen years ago. About why they were listed as killed in action in the first place."

Quot looked puzzled. "Aren't you with the CIA?"

"No."

"What made you come looking for me?"

"You helped run interference for CIA projects in Vietnam."

"Who told you that."

Not wanting to mention McFee's name, Bolan stated half a truth. "I was there."

Quot squinted. "I don't recognize the face."

"It took me a while to get used to it, too."

"You're working for the government?"

"Not for the CIA."

Quot licked his lips. "Who are you working for?"

"No one you know."

"What kind of connections does your control have?"

How much longer would it be until the police arrived? Bolan knew that even with all the strings Brognola had, getting taken in by the SFPD for questioning would take up too much precious time. And it would expose the head Fed's private search for the truth behind the killings. At the moment there was no telling how much damage that revelation would do to Brognola's position. In order to pursue the investigation quickly, Bolan knew he would need the intel available through Justice channels.

"I don't have all night," Bolan said. "Talk or I walk out of this room with you in cuffs and hand you over to the police."

"You don't want to do that."

"Convince me."

Quot tossed the knife into a corner of the room. "I know about the guys getting killed."

"And their deaths involve Mad Dog?"

"I don't know. Operation Mad Dog was a CIA plan to get rid of a hit team near the end of American involvement in the war. It failed because Shane Innis was too damn smart for the guys over him who'd thought they were running the Hawks instead of him."

"Who's Innis?" Dim memories rattled around in the back of Bolan's mind. He was sure he'd never met the man, but there was something back there just the same. He just couldn't put his finger on it. There were too many memories, too many wars since then.

"Major Shane Innis. He was leader of the Hawks from the beginning. He's been operating as a mercenary under the name of Timothy Manchester."

"The CIA's trying to kill these men?"

"I don't think the CIA even knew those guys were still alive. Innis covered his tracks well, and he took care of his team. See, that was Hacker's whole problem with Operation Mad Dog—he didn't see the kind of loyalty Innis commanded from his men, or the loyalty Innis got from the control working immediately over him. Innis didn't get out of there alone. He had help."

Bolan held the gun steady as he tried to find a handle on the information Quot was giving him. The name Hacker was ringing bells, too, leaving a sour taste in his mouth. McFee hadn't mentioned the name. Why? Perhaps Hacker had been an alias used by a top CIA man during the war, and the name had as much substance behind it as Lawrence's and Stoddard's. Maybe less.

"Who's Hacker?" Bolan asked.

Quot shook his head. "You've got a preview, G-man, that's all you get. I'm not saying another fucking word until you get me somewhere safe."

A siren screamed into life only a few blocks away.

"Turn around," Bolan commanded. He tried to evaluate his chances of disappearing into the San Francisco night while escorting a prisoner. It didn't look good. The police were searching for him. Quot's surviving gunners would be, too, once they got in touch with other gang members. And possibly the CIA. No. He needed to figure the CIA in. The Agency had been involved in the cover-up for the past fifteen years at least; they wouldn't stop now.

Quot didn't move.

"Turn around," Bolan repeated.

"If you turn me over to the cops, I'll never see the morning. You might as well shoot me now."

"You think the CIA is looking for you?"

"I know they are. Some of my usual information sources into the Agency have gone deaf. It doesn't take a genius to read the writing on the wall."

"Why would they think you're important enough to come looking for?"

"Because I know about Innis and Mad Dog, and they might think I know who's behind the killings."

"You don't think the CIA is?"

"Do you?"

Bolan silently agreed. If the CIA had set the men up for the kill, they wouldn't have made such a production of their deaths. Lawrence and Stoddard would have quietly disappeared, along with however many other men were involved on the wrong side of Mad Dog.

"Do you know who the triggerman is?" Bolan asked.

"I think I can guess, which is more than Hacker or the CIA or even Innis can do at this point."

"Turn around." Bolan held up a pair of handcuffs.

"You're making a mistake," Quot said as he turned to face the wall.

"I think I am, too," Bolan replied as he snapped the handcuffs into place, "because I'm going to try to take you out of here with me."

A ruby pinpoint of light flickered to life against Quot's shoulder. Bolan yanked on the chain between the cuffs as he watched the ruby dot dart to Quot's temple. Before the man's body could react to the abrupt force of the Executioner's tug, Quot's head exploded into dozens of bloody fragments.

The corpse followed Bolan down as spinning pieces of the shattered window spilled across the wooden floor. Releasing his grisly burden, Bolan kicked out for the safety of the hallway as bullets rapidly trailed the dancing ruby dot that tried to catch up to him.

He paused in the hallway at a window that overlooked the alley behind the building, pushed it open and pulled himself over the edge. He let himself down as far as his arms would reach, then dropped. Rolling when he hit the pavement, he came to his feet immediately as he got his bearings. Then he moved out, figuring he'd at least see the face of one of his enemies tonight.

THE CRUSHING PAIN in Talbot's chest helped him struggle back to consciousness. He coughed and wheezed as he searched for his dropped gun, considering it a victory when he raised himself to his knees. He sucked in a deep breath. God, it hurt, hurt worse than he ever thought it would.

He touched the bulletproof vest under his shirt tenderly, finding the flattened slugs from the rifle in an almost even row across his chest. Evidently one had skimmed off the vest, though, because something had dug a small furrow under his left arm just above his elbow. It stung like hell.

Cursing beneath his breath, he tightened his grip on the .45 and made it to his feet. His rapid blinking cleared away some of the fuzzy black patches in front of his eyes. Flames had spread all over the parking area of the building after the explosion. Most of the evidence in there would be destroyed by the fire, he thought, then looked at the bodies lying around him, realizing what was left would take the criminal investigation teams hours to sort out.

Remembering the man in the three-piece suit, Talbot pushed himself into a staggering run as he heard the first approaching siren. Where was Belasko?

Shots rang out, and he glanced up to see a rifle barrel sticking out of a second-story window of the building across the street. Where was the goddamn car?

Wheezing and gasping, holding his hand to his chest as the pain clutched again and again at his lungs, Talbot paused under the window.

The rifle had disappeared from sight.

Talbot blinked his eyes to clear away perspiration, then removed his hand from his chest. If he could find the car, he was sure he could find the men. Then maybe he could make some sense out of everything that had happened. The two guys in the vehicle were government issue. Talbot was sure of that. They had the feel about them that Belasko had been lacking, that almost unendurable arrogance that Talbot had encountered once before during a murder investigation.

Sounds echoed in the alley. A siren died out on the street, but Talbot was far enough into the alley that he couldn't see the cruiser.

He found the car parked behind the building. Trying to forget about the drumbeats of pain rocking his chest, Talbot wrapped both hands around the automatic, then took a step forward. Even before he reached the sedan he could see that it was empty.

Footsteps rattled on the fire escape above him. Retreating under the metal stairs, Talbot let the breath ease out of his lungs, feeling his heart step up the tempo. These guys, whoever they were and whoever they ultimately worked for, wouldn't hesitate to kill him. They'd already proved that. Maybe the guy with the rifle had taken Belasko out.

Talbot felt fear inch its way into his stomach, tasting cold bile. The footsteps coming down the fire escape were almost directly above him. Would the shadows gathered there be enough to conceal him? Then he could see the backs of the man's legs descending the series of steps in front of him.

The fear was an old thing, a haunting echo of the first time he'd gone into a residence when he was in uniform. Anything could happen when a cop walked into somebody's house; the possibilities were endless. A cop was a cop no matter what, and the uniform all too often turned out to be a target for abuse, anger and physical attack. Invited or not, every time a policeman answered a call to enter someone's house, that policeman was rolling the bones to see what happened.

The thought was always in Talbot's head when he found himself in the middle of a situation he couldn't understand. Like now. The fear was also part of the attraction of the job. The not knowing. He'd found himself drawn to it from the very first. Captivated. Like a moth to an open flame.

So far he hadn't been burned, but he'd been lucky.

The man double-timed it down the last few steps, reaching into a coat pocket. Keys jangled and glinted as they came free in his hand. Talbot didn't see a gun. He reached out a big hand and wrapped his fingers in the material of the man's shirt, yanking with every ounce of his 242 pounds. The guy almost came off his feet, losing the keys somewhere in a gleaming butterfly of movement. Talbot didn't stop pulling until the man slammed facefirst into the brick wall. Then he grabbed the man's shirt collar and forced him to his knees, moaning and holding his face.

They didn't teach karate in the neighborhood where Talbot grew up, but a guy wouldn't have time for all that yelling and posturing shit anyway. Back home, when you took a guy out, you took him out fast because you could always figure he had friends with him.

Just like now.

Cold metal touched the back of Talbot's neck.

"Drop the gun," a cold voice ordered.

Swallowing hard, Talbot let the .45 fall, flinching mentally at the damage the pavement probably did to the finish of the pistol.

The first man was still on his knees, rocking with the pain. Blood shone wet and dark on his fingers. Talbot felt the other man's gun trace a half circle against his neck as the man came around to face him.

The gunner was five-ten, about 170 pounds, dark hair, dark eyes, late twenties. A rifle was slung across his back.

Talbot's mind cataloged the information automatically even though he was sure he'd never see the man again. One way or another.

The man reached out and tapped Talbot on the chest, a shark's grin twisting his thin lips. The gun never slipped, not even against the slick film of perspiration Talbot knew was covering him. "Vest, huh?" the man said.

Talbot remained silent. The pressure of the gun against his neck was like a challenge, taunting him to test his reflexes against those of the man who held it.

"Should have figured you for a vest," the man went on. He raised his voice. "Are you okay, Billy?"

The kneeling man mumbled something that Talbot couldn't understand.

"Go get in the car, Billy. I'll be along in a minute as soon as I take care of business here." A smile flickered under the man's flat, dark eyes.

Talbot swallowed, feeling the muzzle of the gun throb against his Adam's apple. When the gunshot cracked like a double thunderclap, he closed his eyes involuntarily, his breath catching at the back of his throat. He couldn't feel the gun anymore.

Then he opened his eyes and saw the man's body sprawled in front of him. The top of the guy's head had been blown off. Scooping the .38 from his hip, Talbot whirled and dropped to one knee to cover the mouth of the alley.

Belasko was centered in the open sights of the .38. God, he almost hadn't recognized the man in time. He opened his eyes as he lowered the revolver's barrel from the Justice man's chest, not putting it away because he didn't feel that secure.

Jerking the survivor to his feet, Talbot threw the man across the hood of the sedan and buried the barrel of the

.38 just under the guy's ear. He retrieved the handcuffs from the back of his belt and cuffed the man's hands behind his back. Then, looking back at the Justice agent, he tried to equate the dark-garbed man wearing blackface with the man he'd met that morning. There was a general comparison, yes, but this way, the way Belasko was dressed now with the military webbing and the weapons, this way seemed to fit the depth Talbot had sensed in the man from the beginning. It explained the man's organization, the way he assimilated data so quickly, the reason he felt comfortable working alone. Talbot had known guys like him back in the war, guys who went into enemy territory and stayed in deep for long periods at a time. A good man to have at your back, but a bad one to have on your trail. For a moment Talbot felt sorry for the man or men Belasko was tracking, then realized they were probably as bad if not worse than the man who'd tried to kill him.

"You okay?" Talbot asked as he finished cuffing his prisoner.

"Yeah. How about you?"

"Bruised but unbent."

Bolan holstered his weapon and crossed the distance to the dead man. He started going through the man's pockets. "Has your guy got an ID on him?"

"I'll let you know in a minute." Talbot riffled through his captive's clothing, turning up a fold of hundred-dollar bills, some loose change, fingernail clippers, a package of gum, but nothing with a name on it. "Nothing."

"Same here."

Talbot heard the note of disgust in the big man's voice and watched him walk around the car and open the glove compartment. He sat in the passenger seat and went through the vehicle registration.

"Hey," the cuffed man said, struggling to raise his head to look at Bolan. "He isn't a cop. He doesn't have the right to go through that car. I have rights."

Talbot pushed the man into a seated position by the front wheel of the car. "You have rights when I say you have rights."

Bolan made a notation in a small notebook and stuffed the papers back into the glove compartment. "It's a rental. The names probably don't mean anything."

"It means these guys are out-of-town talent," Talbot said. "Which means airports, records and points of origin."

"If it'll do any good." The look on the Justice agent's face was grim and tired, but Talbot could see the mind at work behind the blue eyes, analyzing, concluding, deciding.

"Where's Quot?" Talbot asked.

"In the other building. Second floor. Main office. When your investigation teams take the bullets out of the wall, they'll find the one that killed him. You'll also find it came from the Weatherby strapped across that guy's back."

"What's all this about?" Talbot asked.

Bolan shook his head. "I can't go into it now."

Talbot felt the rage inside him boil over the edge, out of control. "What the hell do you mean you can't go into it?"

"Just what I said. It's nothing personal."

"Like hell! I got guys dropping dead all over my goddamn town! Then I got the Bobbsey Twins here and I don't know if they were after you and Quot got in the way, or if they were after Quot and figured you as a goddamn door prize. Me, they were willing to off because I was an irritation. And you can't tell me anything?"

"What I'm working on has moved out of your town, Sergeant, and out of this state. We got lucky this time. You could have been stretched out on that morgue slab instead of that guy over there. If it involved you any further than this, I'd fill you in. But it doesn't."

Bolan turned and walked toward the opposite end of the alley.

Talbot watched him for a moment, not believing the guy was just going to try to walk away from everything like this. The staccato patter of the cruisers out in the street reached his ears, marching to a familiar cadence. "Belasko!" Talbot called out angrily.

"Take care of yourself, Sergeant."

"You can't just walk away from this, damn it!"

The warrior kept walking and didn't reply.

Talbot raised the .38 and eased the hammer back, knowing the big man could hear the noise it made. "Belasko!" Just before his target rounded the far end of the alley, the detective dropped the revolver to his side and stared at the dead man. Then he loosened his tie and helped his prisoner up. When he looked back at the other end of the alley, Belasko was gone. He didn't know how the big man expected to get out of the area unseen while wearing the blacksuit and weapons, but Talbot had a hunch the guy would manage. He pushed the prisoner ahead of him as he went to join the uniforms, wondering how his chief was going to react to his being involved in a firefight to this degree and not knowing what the hell was going on. Some detective.

6

Greg Bowen snared the phone unerringly in the darkness, stretching across his bed and the woman who shared it.

"Bowen," he answered, willing his conscious mind to engage. He cracked an eyelid and glanced at the clock—2:13 a.m.

"Greg?"

"Yeah, Zack, you got me," he replied as details of his current assignment started filtering through his mind. The Vietnam War Memorial killings. How the hell did Crosby expect him to run a search for a merc leader in Angola from a desk in Langley? Then there was the question of why field agents were addressing the matter on American soil. Crosby had fobbed it off as an in-house project that was to be tightly controlled with no sharing of information with the other agencies involved. Bowen had then proceeded to be the first person Crosby hadn't shared information with, which made him feel like a lamb being led to slaughter if whatever he was actually supposed to be working on blew up in his face.

"You told me you wanted me to call you the minute something broke on this War Memorial killing thing."

"Right."

"So here I am, and you aren't going to believe this."

"What have you got, Zack?"

"A guy in prison in Leavenworth called the Agency and wants a meet with the section chief ramrodding the investigation."

Synapses started connecting in Bowen's head. He felt wide awake. For almost two weeks he'd been working on this thing in the dark, poking and prodding the reports he'd been given by at least a dozen agents to make sense of the puzzle. In the end, once he'd compiled all the raw data and converted it for easy consumption, he made his report to Crosby, who would come back with follow-up orders. If any. Most of the project seemed to be a process of sitting back and waiting. But Bowen had the impression he wasn't seeing all the reports and that Crosby wasn't limiting himself to waiting.

"What did this guy say, Zack?"

"That he wants to talk."

"How do you know this guy is on the up-and-up?"

"If the call was a phony, it wouldn't have reached me, Greg. The guy knew names."

"What names?"

"Not over the phone, bud."

The woman rolled over in bed, resting a plump breast on Bowen's arm. She looked at him expectantly, eyes gleaming.

Bowen covered the mouthpiece for a moment and said, "Could I have a cigarette, Cyn?"

The woman raised an arched eyebrow and gave him a curious smile as she took a cigarette pack and lighter from the night table. Bowen wasn't surprised; he knew she was aware he didn't smoke.

"The guy give his name?"

Papers rattled on the other end of the connection. "Yeah. Ellston. Steve Ellston. He gave me another name, too—Clark Bonner. He said I could find it on the Vietnam War Memorial."

"And?"

"It's there, amigo."

The lighter flared to life in Bowen's hand. He sucked on the cigarette, focusing on the orange coal at the end, feeling the smoke bite deep. "Did you put a tracer on the call?"

"First thing. It traces directly back to Leavenworth."

"How did the guy get access to a phone this late?"

"You know how it is in prison. If a guy has the bankroll, he can get damn near anything he wants except out."

"Yeah, well, 'out' is what it sounds like this guy wants."

"That's the trade he wants. He tells you what he knows about the guys who have been killed and why, and you pull the right strings to cut him loose."

"He's got to know I can't promise anything like that."

"That's the deal, Greg. He said if you can't come across or get somebody to come across for you, he won't be talking to us. He said he'd start first thing in the morning setting up interviews with everybody from the *Washington Post* down to the *Enquirer*."

"This guy doesn't sound too stable, Zack."

"The problem is, this Ellston or Bonner or whatever the hell his name really is, sounds like a stable guy. He arranged a telephone call tonight, didn't he?"

"Yeah. Did he say why he didn't call during business hours? The warden would have let him."

"This case doesn't really belong to the CIA, remember? The FBI and Justice guys are supposed to be conducting the whole investigation with our informational help. We're not supposed to be fielding teams ourselves."

"But we both know we are, Zack."

"Right."

"And Ellston believes the CIA will be more understanding than any of the other law-enforcement agencies involved."

"My impression of the conversation was that Ellston *knows* the Agency has more to hide on this one."

"And he wants me?"

"Yeah."

"Why didn't he want Crosby? Everybody involved on our team knows Crosby is swinging the ax on this one."

"I mentioned Crosby. I figured it might be a way to take some heat off of you. Didn't mean anything personal by it." Zack sounded uncomfortable.

Imagining the older agent at his desk pushing the papers around with a nervous pencil eraser, Bowen didn't make an issue of the break in the chain of command. He knew the man still had occasional problems taking orders from a much younger section chief. "Did he have a problem with Crosby?"

"Apparently a big one. He claimed Crosby knows a guy named Hacker, and Hacker knows him. Ellston says Hacker's the guy who wants him dead."

"Who's Hacker?"

"I don't know, Chief. I never heard the name before tonight."

"And Ellston gave you no idea of what this is all about?"

"No. He just says there's more guys marked to die and he's afraid he's one of them."

"Why?"

"Ellston wouldn't say."

Cyn traced the underside of Bowen's jaw as he thought. It figured that, after a week of pursuing the woman and finally talking her into his bed, something like this would happen. He gazed at her in the darkness, remembering the lines and planes of her naked body. She was a new waitress in the coffee shop he frequented when he was in Langley, a big blond girl from Texas who liked to laugh.

"What have we got on Ellston, Zack?"

"He's finishing up the last three months of a six-month sentence for assaulting an officer."

"Any priors?"

"No. According to the file, Steven J. Ellston is clean except for this one indiscretion."

"Amazing," Bowen said wryly. "It takes a fistful of balls to hit a cop."

"That's what I thought."

"What about military experience?"

"None."

"Check under the Bonner name."

Computer keys clacked in Bowen's ear.

"Yeah, he was in Vietnam, Greg, but I don't know what he did. Somebody has a lock on the information."

"Us?"

"Yes."

"The same lock as on the other two?"

"Affirmative."

"Terrific." Bowen stubbed out the cigarette.

"You'll like this, too. Bonner's enlistment in the Army was in deferment of a prison term in '63."

"What was the charge?"

"Hitting a cop."

"This guy seems to run true to form, doesn't he?"

"Experienced."

"Maybe too experienced."

"What do you mean?"

Bowen captured Cyn's fingers in his hand to stop the movement. "The clean slate stands out. Ellston sounds like a troublemaker. I'm having a hard time believing this is his first offense in twenty-six years."

"I see what you mean."

"How much longer did you say he had?"

"Three months."

"What about parole?"

"He turned it down."

"Doesn't that sound strange to you, Zack?"

"Maybe there was a reason."

"Yeah. Maybe the reason was parole officers. If he kicked back and did his full time, there wouldn't be anybody looking over his shoulder when he got out. He might even have a new name waiting for him when the doors opened."

Zack grunted.

"How soon can you get me a plane to Leavenworth?"

"It'll be waiting on you."

"Do me one other favor."

"What?"

"Don't tell Crosby about this until he gets there in the morning."

There was a hesitation, then, "Okay."

Bowen said thanks and hung up.

"Problems?" Cyn asked.

"I've got to go."

She looked away from him, pulling the covers up to hide her nudity.

"I'm sorry, babe."

"It's okay," she said, though she sounded upset. "I'm beginning to get used to the wham-bam-thank-you-ma'am attitude you find here in the East."

"You don't have to go, Cyn. Stay here. As soon as I'm back, I'll give you a call. Shouldn't be gone more than a day." Bowen felt like shit. Through his high school years he must have had a callused heart or something, because he could rip off a standard parting lie with the best of them. Or maybe, since joining the Agency at twenty-one, he'd learned how fragile love and trust really were, and how little of it you really found in the world. He kissed her and was glad when she kissed back. He levered himself out of bed. "I meant what I said."

"I'm going to hold you to it, cowboy," she said with the smile that had first made him interested in her.

He switched on the shower, then remembered he'd forgotten a towel. When he stepped into the bedroom, Cyn was just putting the phone down. Warnings twinged inside Bowen's stomach, intensified reactions that matched the ones he'd experienced since taking over the Vietnam Memorial killings as section chief and not being given any information to work with or even the reason why the CIA was involved. For one frozen moment his eyes locked with the woman's, and he saw a deepness there he hadn't expected.

"I was just calling time and temperature," Cyn said as she rolled over to the middle of the bed. "You're going to need a coat." She smiled.

Bowen nodded, not trusting himself to speak, then got a towel. He shaved quickly, staring into the dark eyes reflected in the steam-covered mirror, asking himself why he had been naive enough to believe his own Agency would play fair with him in whatever cover-up was being concocted by Crosby when every other department involved was fair game.

His hand shook as he finished shaving and thought about the real identity of the girl in the next room. He nicked himself twice and blood ran eagerly down his throat from the self-inflicted wounds. For a moment he wondered if worse was to come.

MACK BOLAN STOOD by the pay phone on the wall outside the twenty-four-hour laundry just off Kearny Street, waiting for Brognola to return his call from a safe phone in D.C. He finished the dregs of the first cup of black coffee he'd purchased from a vending machine inside, tossed it into the wastebasket near the phone and reached for the second cup. He knew he'd have to stop for something to eat soon, before the caffeine jitters ran rampant in him.

Things were starting to come to a head on the current operation. He could feel it. The people involved in the cover-up were starting to make mistakes. The move to eliminate Quot had been staged too late in the game to keep injury from being done. He was sure Talbot wouldn't be able to hold the man taken prisoner for long, but it was sure to tip many more people to the fact that the CIA was taking a cut of the action.

Bolan assumed Quot's death sentence had come about because of the Warrior's involvement with a crack dealer. Probably someone in Langley had tapped a sensitive trigger to Quot's name and when McFee pulled the file earlier that morning, it had sent out signals to whoever was monitoring the man.

The Executioner felt no remorse over Gung Quot's death. The Vietnamese had been a death dealer himself, visiting slow execution to everyone who touched his merchandise. If the CIA hit team hadn't taken the man out, Bolan would have done it for them. That was one thing Sergeant Talbot had been right about: balking in the middle of what appeared to be a preemptive strike would have opened the doors for a tidal wave of blood that would have washed over the city.

Now, with Quot and his organization broken, there would be a natural void the other crack dealers would move in to fill. During this movement Talbot and other members of the SFPD would be able to place undercover officers within strategic offices of the drug trade, perhaps eventually crippling or destroying it. Especially when Bolan gave the big homicide cop his farewell presents: Tiep and the intel he'd put together from infiltrating the DiCarlo regime.

The phone rang when Bolan was halfway through his second cup of coffee.

"Striker?"

"Yeah, Hal." Bolan gave the big Fed a thumbnail sketch of the night's activities.

"You're sure those guys were CIA?"

"I'm sure."

"Damn. And we still have no idea what this is all about?"

"No, but we do have more to go on now. Quot mentioned an operation by the CIA near the end of American involvement in Vietnam. Something called Mad Dog." Bolan paused to glance at the young man and woman folding clothes at a table inside the laundry. The young couple looked tired, but they frequently laughed at what they each had to say. His attention drifted away from the window as he heard Brognola's pen scratch against a notepad on the other end of the connection. "According to Quot, there was a Major Shane Innis who led a group called the Hawks that operated under the direction of the CIA. The control for the group was somebody named Hacker. I've got a feel for both names, Hal, and I don't get a good scan on either of them."

"Where did Quot fit in?"

"As a liaison for the South Vietnamese."

"So the CIA killed him because he knew about Mad Dog and these two guys?"

"It looks that way."

"But, assuming this is all part of a scrub mission that's running fifteen years late, why would the CIA want to announce its intention to the rest of the guys involved?"

"I don't think the CIA is behind the murders."

"Then who is?"

"I don't know yet. Quot told me he thought he knew who the triggerman was, and the way he said it led me to believe the person wasn't connected through Langley. Another point is that Quot might have gone into deeper cover if he knew the Agency was setting up to take him out. But he hadn't dropped out of sight. He thought his connections to the CIA were solid. They'd carried him through the past fifteen years. My intel was that Quot was also used as a CIA connection on some Asian strikes."

"It figures, Striker." Brognola's voice was gruff.

Bolan knew the head Fed was upset. Brognola had made his choice years ago to go after life, liberty and the pursuit of happiness through the established channels of the Justice Department, and to finding a way through the red tape of the legal system that became more intricate with each passing year. Brognola believed in the system, which made it sometimes hard to step across the line to injure the credibility of other American agencies who were more than merely circumspect with their dealings. That was where the major differences between Bolan and Brognola evolved—there in the gray middle ground of right and wrong. The Executioner drew a hard line between the two, with no legal loopholes. His system was birthed in cold, hard fact, midwifed with a true justice blind to buy-offs and a legal system that had been turned to Swiss cheese by politicians and lawyers, and grew to retribution in the hellgrounds he tended. Where Brognola believed in the systems of the United States, Bolan believed in the American spirit.

"Lie down with dogs..." Brognola said, and let the thought trail off.

"There might be a lot of people with dirty hands on this one, Hal," Bolan said.

"I know." Brognola sighed.

Bolan heard a grinding noise and knew the big man was chewing an antacid tablet. That was another difference between him and his friend. True, he might make a fatal slip one day when faced with an enemy, but it would be the enemy who would take him down. Brognola had to put himself against the enemy and the wearing-down factors of the system itself. Even calling Bolan in to help when something went clearly beyond the scope of the things Justice could handle wore on Brognola.

"In fifteen years' time, I wouldn't be surprised to find how high up this thing goes."

"You might not want to know."

"Thinking of the Man?"

"His tour of duty as the director of the CIA was from 1976 to 1977. Operation Mad Dog was scheduled for 1975. Assuming the files weren't closed on the project immediately after our involvement in the Vietnam War, he could have known about it."

"That question might come up even if he's innocent, Striker."

"I know."

"Any plans on how you're going to handle it?"

"I've met the Man, Hal. I believe in him. I'll stand beside him on this because I don't think he knew anything about Mad Dog."

"The problem is, the Man could have advisers working with him right now who were involved. Hacker doesn't ring any bells for me, either, but it sounds like an alias. This guy might be in deep right now."

"Then, when the time comes—if it becomes necessary—I'll remove him."

"Striker...."

Bolan waited, knowing there was nothing Brognola could say. Hal was a friend, a good friend. Maybe the closest thing to a friend Bolan had ever or would ever know. They were both aware of that. But Brognola had asked for Bolan's help in the matter, knowing in the Executioner's battles there were no halfway measures.

The big Fed cancelled the thought with a sigh. "I'll get the Bear on these names as soon as I clear the phone."

"Add Timothy Manchester to your list," Bolan said. "Quot told me Innis was using the Manchester name in mercenary work he's involved in now."

"Did he say where the Manchester name was being used?"

"No."

"There are a lot of countries using mercs now, Striker. This could take some time."

"I know. If I can narrow it down for you later, I will."

"Anything else?"

"See if you can get records of the autopsies on the first two guys who were killed."

"Do you have any idea?"

"Just working a hunch. It might not turn out to lead to much."

"What should I be looking for in the reports?"

"Recent scars and injuries. If Innis is operating as a mercenary somewhere, it might be interesting to find out if his men are, too. If we can find a common denominator with their lives in the present, maybe we can track it back to what's going on now."

"I can probably arrange it so you can look at the third guy yourself, Striker."

"Third guy?"

"Yeah. A report crossed my desk about an hour before your call."

"Who is this one?"

There was a pause, and Bolan could hear paper being shuffled.

"Mitch Henderson. A sheriff's deputy in Francis, Oklahoma, found the body earlier this evening. Somebody had pinned a note to his shirt with the name Mike Drake on it."

"And Mike Drake checks out with the other names."

"Correct."

"Who knows about this so far?"

"The Oklahoma State Bureau of Investigation has already checked out the scene and are filing prelim reports. I'll make sure we get one channeled our way, but I thought you might want to take a look at this one firsthand."

"Can you get me a plane?"

"Already waiting for you at San Francisco International."

"What kind of cover do you want me to use down there?"

"Use the Belasko ID. You've already got it."

"The name's getting pretty hot, Hal."

"If you can take the heat, Striker," Brognola said gruffly, "then so can I. Maybe knowing somebody's breathing down their necks will shake these bastards up a little."

"I'll want to talk to the deputy who found the body."

"I'll arrange it. The guy might miss out on a little sleep, but we all are."

"Is there anything new on this one?"

Brognola grunted. "Possibly. We won't know for sure until you get down there and have a look yourself. From the deputy's reports, a few of the townspeople got a look at the guy they think killed Henderson. The descriptions vary, the way you'd expect them to in an investigation like this, but they all agree on one thing—the guy who was checking up on Henderson the day before he got killed was Oriental."

"Vietnamese?"

"Possibly."

Bolan turned the information around and looked at it from every side he could imagine. The only Vietnamese link he'd discovered so far had been the war itself and Quot. Had the CIA hired Quot to free-lance the murders out? Or had Quot tried tracking some of the men down himself for insurance or for some other reason? It had been fifteen years. If the CIA or Quot had possessed information on the men earlier, why would they have waited fifteen years to use it? And why would the CIA terminate Quot if they had hired the man to manage the delayed scrub mission for them? Or was there another reason? Maybe, fifteen years later, the war itself had found a way to follow those men home. The reasoning scanned, but he couldn't make it fit. It would have helped to know what Innis and the others had been doing during the war. But that kind of information was something else he was going to have to dig out for himself.

If he could stay alive long enough to do it.

"Give me a call if you get something going down there," Brognola said.

Bolan promised he would and broke the connection. He walked back into the laundry for two more cups of coffee, aware that the laughter from the young couple died away the instant he entered the room. He knew it was caused by the aura of violence that was an ethereal thing about him.

He carried the coffee to the change machine and broke a five-dollar bill into quarters. He smiled at the girl to relax her, watching one tentatively tug at the corners of her mouth in response. The young man remained holding the girl's arm possessively. They couldn't have named it, but the Executioner knew his action was an innate animal response triggered by the subconscious knowledge of the nearness of a hunter.

Balancing one coffee cup on the pay phone, Bolan tore a circle off the lid of the other, took a sip, then started dropping quarters in the slot as he began tracking Talbot.

SERGEANT TALBOT FELT the coolness of the morgue wrap chill fingers around his body, and he shivered inside his jacket. Three sheet-covered bodies lay on chrome-and-plastic tables in the center of the room, with bloodstains marking the sheets in various places. More bodies were stored down the hall, waiting for the team of coroners that had been called in to work the autopsies.

Talbot stood with his back to a wall, arms across his chest in an effort to stay warm. He nursed the cup of coffee in his hand, letting it warm his palm. He'd called Mandy earlier and explained the situation, without telling her that he'd gotten locked into the whole affair through his own curiosity and reluctance to let things slide. But somehow he had the impression she knew what had really happened. Still, she seemed more relieved that he hadn't been hurt than she was upset that he wouldn't be coming home for a while. He hadn't told her about the arm wound. Yet.

He sipped more coffee, watching the sheet-covered figure on the nearest table. The CIA agent who'd tried to kill him was under that one, and that particular corpse was the only one he was interested in. The other men he knew, more or less. This man was an enigma.

As Belasko was.

He cursed himself again for letting the big man walk away. But what choice had the man given him? Talbot couldn't have shot the guy in the back. And Belasko had saved his life on top of that. The whole thing was screwy from start to finish. Only Talbot had the impression the thing didn't finish here. San Francisco had been a way station for something bigger. But what? He wondered if he would ever know.

The other man who had been with the sniper was in a holding cell downtown and hadn't said a word since he'd been placed in the back of a cruiser.

Talbot had figured there would be more answers here, with the dead man, and had driven himself to the morgue. It was better than hanging around the crime scene arguing with Varrick about how the analysis teams were supposed to operate. And there hadn't been a lot left on the first floor to investigate.

The door opened and Dr. Chin entered. The pathologist squinted a couple of times behind his black-framed glasses and smoothed at imaginary wrinkles in his white lab smock. "Detective Talbot," he said, "there's a call for you on line 3."

"Thanks, George," the detective replied, then scooped up the receiver on the wall and punched the flashing button. "Talbot."

"How's the arm?"

Talbot recognized the voice immediately. "Fine." He tried to keep his frustration in, not wanting to blow it if Belasko had changed his mind about letting him in on what was going on.

"Two things," Belasko said. "First, I've got Tiep in protective custody."

Talbot took a pad from his jacket pocket and wrote the address down, wincing as the pain from his arm reacted to the movement.

"The men there are under orders to release him to you and no one else. Tiep will help you finish breaking Quot's supply ring down."

"What makes you so sure? Tiep doesn't have a reputation for being the most congenial of criminals."

"We talked. I told him he'd rather do business with you than me. He agreed."

Talbot agreed, too, but he didn't say anything.

"The second thing is that there's a key taped to the underside of your desk that fits a bus locker at AC Transit. You'll find information inside the locker that covers everything I could turn up on Carm DiCarlo's connections. With a little work, I think a smart cop could take the stuff I detailed out and run with it."

"And you think I'm it?"

"I know you are," Bolan replied, and broke the connection.

Talbot slammed the phone back into its cradle. Then he looked around to see if anyone had noticed. His audience hadn't moved under their respective sheets. Loose ends, and now it looked as if Belasko was going to be one forever, as well as whatever it was that had brought the man to San Francisco in the first place.

He lifted the receiver and dialed the detectives' squad room. Raymond answered on the second ring. "Alex, what have they got on the guy I brought in?"

"Nothing. The guy's already been released from custody."

Another wave of anger surged through Talbot. "How the hell did that happen? The man hadn't even been booked yet."

"You'll have to ask the chief, Whit. It was his order."

"Shit."

"That's what I said. This guy had an attitude, I promise."

"Did he call anybody while he was there?"

"No. He hadn't been booked. He didn't even ask to use a phone. Who was this guy, Whit?"

"Would you believe CIA?"

"No shit?"

"No shit."

"Must be organization if they can pull you out of the soup that fast."

"Yeah, well, I got one of the bastards over here that ain't so lucky."

"I'll see if I can find out who talked to the chief."

"Do that." Talbot replaced the phone, staring at the dead man. Son of a bitch. These guys could shoot a cop with intent to kill and walk away from it unscathed an hour later. How the hell did you fight something like that? He glanced at the wide and long blood spot that soaked the upper part of the sheet, thinking Belasko might definitely have one method.

Dr. Chin reentered the room, making notations on a clipboard.

"Hey, George, how much longer will it be before you can start on this guy?" Talbot asked.

"Which one is this?"

"He didn't have any ID."

Dr. Chin moved to the table and pulled the sheet back. Talbot felt his stomach rumble threateningly when he looked at the hollow cavity surrounded by jagged edges at the top of the corpse's head.

"Ah, yes," Dr. Chin said, drawing up the sheet again. "We won't be doing this one, Whit."

"What do you mean?"

Dr. Chin shrugged his narrow shoulders. "I mean someone called Dr. Farrell, and our office was instructed not to touch this guy. Someone is supposed to come for the body soon."

"Who called Farrell?"

The coroner looked annoyed. "I don't know, Whit. I don't make the rules. I just play by them." He closed the clipboard and walked back out the door.

Talbot cursed the corpse under his breath, remembering how the bullets had thudded painfully into his chest. It would have been him lying there on this table if it hadn't been for the Kevlar vest and, later, Belasko.

Glancing around the room, he spotted a ceramic coffee cup with George Chin's name on it sitting on one of the tables. Talbot dropped his disposable cup into a waste bin, then he swiped the cup from the table and took it to a hand sink built into one wall. He emptied it, then washed and dried it carefully, taking pains to touch only the inside of the cup as he carried it to the dead agent.

Steeling himself, Talbot took the fingers in his hand and—one by one—pressed each onto the surface of the coffee cup. The ceramic surface would hold the prints until he could have them lifted later. Then maybe he'd get lucky and be able to get hold of a name.

Once he finished, he opened some of the drawers beneath the autopsy tables and rummaged around until he found a carton of plastic bags used for taking specimens from the corpses. He put the coffee cup in one, then tucked the whole thing into a side pocket of his jacket.

He had just resumed leaning up against the wall when Dr. Chin reentered the room, followed by a pair of men who looked like carbon copies of the corpse. The coroner pointed out the body and they placed it on the gurney they were pushing.

"Where are his personal effects?" one of them asked.

"In my office," Dr. Chin replied. "Follow me and I'll get them for you."

Talbot followed the group out of the room, noticing the hard-eyed look the men were giving him. He ignored them and walked toward the building's entrance.

GREG BOWEN STARED at the swinging body inside the cell, suspended by what looked like a pair of shoestrings from high-top tennis shoes. The guard beside him cursed and radioed the jailer to open the cell door.

The electronic lock snicked open and the door slid back on its own. The gray light of dawn was starting to creep into the cell block, lending the metal cages a surrealistic look that cut into Bowen's sensibilities. He'd visited prisons before, in several cities as well as a handful of countries, and he'd always been overwhelmed by the hopelessness he found there.

Bowen followed the guard into the cell, listening to the broad man warn the other cellmate to stay on the bed. Bowen had left his gun at the check-in point and felt naked somehow without it. Especially here. Especially now.

He gripped the hanging man's waist quickly, taking the weight from the guy's neck, knowing it was already too late but doing it just the same. The other prisoners in the cell block were starting to wake now, demanding in loud, raucous voices to know what was going on.

The guard clambered on the lower bunk and reached out for the shoestrings. "Christ, Christ, Christ." The guard's words sounded like a litany. His fingers dug frantically at the knotted length until it came loose.

Bowen went down with the sudden weight, scrambling until he could work on the knots at the back of the man's neck. The prisoner's eyes were glazed, his tongue protruding. The shoestrings came loose in Bowen's fingers. He checked the carotid artery and found no pulse.

The guard started to administer CPR, but the CIA agent knew it was a waste of time. "Is this Ellston?" Bowen asked.

The guard nodded, still pumping away at the dead man's sternum in the standard hand-over-hand procedure. Down the hall a small phalanx of uniformed prison guards had been ushered into the cell block by the man at the checkpoint. They ran toward the cell.

Bowen looked at the cell's only other resident: a big black man whose hair had turned iron-gray with age. His arms looked fat, but they were tight with corded muscle.

"I don't suppose you know anything about this?" Bowen asked.

The man shook his head and smiled, revealing a gap where his four front teeth should have been. "Man be upset about his lot in life," the man said. "Some people, they be weak. Can't take livin' inside a cage."

"And you expect us to believe Ellston here took his own life?"

"Believe what you want to, 'cause you goin' to anyway. I learn that a long time ago. Man be despondent, that's all."

"Bullshit," Bowen said.

The big man ignored him, still wearing a smile on his huge-jowled face. Bowen strode out of the cell, brushing past the crowd of men clustered around the body and drawing hostile stares. He felt the hot eyes of the prisoners around the cell block on him as he tried to sort things out. But everything was all jumbled, tumbled rocky and jagged in his mind. He didn't know what was going on. Only that he was being set up to take a fall.

Ellston had refused to go to Crosby because he had been afraid of the man. Obviously with good reason. But who was Crosby fronting for? Bowen asked himself. Crosby was with the old school of the CIA, with a lot of the men who had been involved in the Vietnamese covert actions. These men who were being killed were tied into that somehow.

But how?

Bowen had the feeling he wasn't meant to find out. He was being used as a stalking-horse and as a scapegoat. Maybe there were others like Ellston, men who would come forward if they felt they could talk to someone who would protect them from whatever vengeance was being visited on them. His appointment to the project might draw those men out, make them vulnerable to Crosby or whoever it was that was keeping his actions under surveillance.

He remembered the phone call Cyn had made, wondering if it had been her or Zack who had tipped Crosby off. He couldn't trust his own department. So where did that leave him? And how long would he be safe there? He wished he had a cigarette almost as much as he wished he had an answer.

7

"This is where we found the body," Deputy Wayne Barnowski said, indicating the general area with a scuffed boot toe.

Bolan knelt, eyeing the lay of the land and searching for a feel about the place. The turgid brown waters of the South Canadian River rolled westerly to his left. To his right tree branches grew into a latticework that formed a natural canopy over the steep incline that had been worn smooth in places by two- and four-wheeled all-terrain vehicles. Creepers, vines, weeds and grass covered the rest of the topography, coming to a stop only a few feet deep into the sandy area where Barnowski stood.

"This wasn't where Henderson was killed," Bolan said, squinting through the treetops at the afternoon sun.

The big deputy shook his head and spit a yellowing brown glob of tobacco juice into the sand near his feet. He automatically covered it over with his boot. Barnowski was a tall man, with broad shoulders that narrowed down to a lean waist. He wore a sweat-stained Stetson, blue jeans, a blue Chambray work shirt and a faded jean jacket that showed the wear and tear caused by long hours of sun and rain. A well-used Sam Browne belt held a Dan Wesson .357 Magnum. Despite the last name, Barnowski was a full-blooded Choctaw Indian and had a lot of mannerisms that reminded Bolan of PenTeam Able's point man, Loudelk.

Loudelk had displayed the same slow amiability when in the company of strangers, but it had been a guise that kept his enemies off balance so that they didn't know the full danger of the man they faced.

Bolan got the same impression about Barnowski.

"No. Henderson was killed up that incline." Barnowski pointed up one of the barren strips cutting a swath through the foliage.

Bolan pushed himself to his feet and walked toward the incline, feeling his booted feet sink into the sand. "Who found the body?"

"A couple of kids who came out last night to ride their dirt bikes and drink beer." Barnowski followed, keeping his hands tucked in his jeans pockets.

"Did they see anyone out here?"

"Nope."

"What did they see?" Bolan stopped at the top of the incline and looked back down. From his vantage point he had a more or less unobstructed view in all directions. If Henderson had been part of a covert military group operating under the CIA in Vietnam, how had the man let himself be taken?

Barnowski leaned against a tall oak tree. "They saw Henderson's pickup parked where we left mine. Then they saw his body."

"What kind of man was Mitch Henderson?"

Barnowski regarded Bolan with a flat brown stare. "Don't rightly know. This here's a big county, mister, and the Sheriff's Department stays busy what with one thing and then another."

"Does the town have a local cop?"

Shaking his head, Barnowski said, "I'm about as local as they get. Francis is a small town, and you don't get a lot of trouble out here that the local folk don't take care of

ABLE TEAM
DICK STIVERS
GAR WILSON
GULF OF FIRE
PHOENIX FORCE
VIETNAM: GROUND ZERO
MACV
DON PENDLETON'S #129
THE EXECUTIONER
FEATURING MACK BOLAN

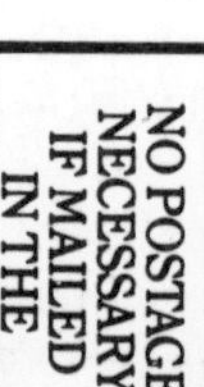

NO POSTAGE
NECESSARY
IF MAILED
IN THE
UNITED STATES

themselves. Oh, they've had some grief from their kids off and on, and a handful of rowdies that had to be dressed down. But nothing like this."

"You mean nothing like murder?"

Barnowski pushed his hat back with a thumb and squatted. He sorted through the underbrush around the tree and came up with two empty shell casings. They sparkled bright gold against the nut-brown of his skin. "Oh, they have a murder now and again, but not this kind." He rolled the casings back and forth across his palm. "These are 9 mm casings, mister, from an automatic weapon. Course, I'm sure that's no surprise to you. You seem like a man who knows what he's looking for."

"What," Bolan agreed, "but not who or why."

"That the honest answer, mister, or you figure on telling me to mind my own business in a nice way?"

Bolan grinned, at ease with the harsh grittiness of the big deputy. "No, that's the truth."

Barnowski nodded and pocketed the brass. "I heard they got a lock on Henderson's other name at the Pentagon."

"Yes."

"You care to unlock it for me?"

"I was hoping you could help me do that for myself."

The echoing caw of a crow reached the riverbanks and reverberated for a moment before fading away. The deputy appeared to be considering Bolan's words. Red glared from the whites of his eyes, showing his lack of sleep. He raked a forefinger inside his jawline and dug out the chew of tobacco, then sighed and settled against the tree. Barnowski took his hat off, perched it on a tree limb, then ran a scarred hand through his coal-black hair. "Ain't nobody confirmed it yet, but I think Henderson was one of them Vietnam War Memorial killings."

"I'll confirm it for you," Bolan said. He met the big man's straightforward gaze, willing himself to maintain a sharp edge despite the relaxing effects of the dappled sunshine and the tree-covered land that covered this part of southeastern Oklahoma. He'd been to Oklahoma City before and had been expecting more of the barren flatness he'd found around the metro area instead of the forests of short, squatty trees he'd discovered after landing at a small commercial field north of Ada. Barnowski had been quietly reserved the entire twelve-mile trip down Highway 99 and the annex road to the smaller town.

"I spent most of the night with some government asshole last night," Barnowski said, "which is why my butt is dragging right now. You could say I wasn't overly excited when the sheriff sent somebody to roust me out of bed again later this morning."

Bolan didn't say anything. Barnowski knew it came with the job and didn't need anyone to tell him that.

"This other guy did everything but call me a liar about how much I knew concerning Henderson's murder."

"Not very professional," Bolan said dryly.

"A big-city asshole," Barnowski agreed. "As a result, I got to where I didn't want to give him the time of day. He had access to more information than I had, and he was giving me shit because he was having a bad time of it. If the sheriff hadn't been there, I'd have taken the son of a bitch out here and 'accidently' lost his ass in the brush." The deputy took a can of Prince Albert from his pocket and some papers. He tapped tobacco onto the papers and rolled two cigarettes, offering one to Bolan.

Bolan declined and Barnowski fired his smoke.

He snapped the lighter shut. "Reason I'm telling you this is because you seem like a level guy. Professional, sure, and you probably seen more city life than country life the way we live it out here. And I also figure you for some time spent in the jungle."

"I lived there awhile," Bolan agreed.

"Me, too. Marines for a four-year hitch close to the end of the war, then some time with Air America till I finally got sick enough of the fighting to come home." Barnowski blew smoke. "This asshole I met last night, he reminded me a lot of the CIA pukes behind the Air America operations. Lotta bad memories. He didn't know it, but he was kind of a losing proposition going in. You know what I mean?"

"Yeah," Bolan said. "Did you get a name on the guy?"

"Not one that would do you any good. I already had it checked through a friend of mine. Got a stone wall placed at the end of it that I can't get through."

"Maybe I can come up with something."

Barnowski nodded and flashed a white, mirthless grin. "Maybe you can. But we're going to do a little horse-trading before I tell you anything. We got a custom out here, sort of a game only most of the old-timers know about nowadays. Two guys get together and trade knives, each holding his own knife in one hand while holding the other hand out for the other guy's knife. Time comes, they drop the knives in each other's hand without looking. Then they find out who got the better deal. Problem here is, we can't take what we know and hold it out for the other to take."

Bolan started talking. He'd dealt with other officers of the law like Wayne Barnowski, honest men who pinned their lives behind the badge instead of just a shirt. And he'd found them in three-piece business suits with a twice-a-day shaving habit and in jeans with hair past their shoulders. A good cop didn't come in any particular make or model, and the Executioner had learned to recognize them by the way they held their eyes or the way they stated their points of view.

He told Barnowski everything he knew about the War Memorial murders, withholding only the names of Quot and the men the crack dealer had implicated.

The big deputy had picked up a stick somewhere in the middle of Bolan's dissertation and had started drawing geometric figures in the black soil that capped the incline. Bolan didn't once think the man wasn't paying attention to him.

"You're a fair man, Mr. Belasko," the deputy said. He pulled out his makings and rolled another cigarette.

"I am when I can be."

"Now, I'm going to tell you a story, and you can stop me if you got any questions. I ain't quite as good as you are in summin' things up."

"Good enough."

"A lot of people around here knew Mitch Henderson," the deputy said, putting his stick away. "I talked to five men down to the café this morning while I was filing my report. One of them was the town gunsmith, and he figures he talked to Henderson more'n any man in town."

"Henderson was interested in guns."

"Right. The problem is, none of these guys knew Henderson's business. He's been living in Francis a lotta years now, and he's managed to keep to himself and to keep his neighbors from finding out what he does with himself, which is impressive as hell in a small town like this. Me, I got neighbors who could tell you when I was born and when I was married."

Bolan smiled in spite of the seriousness of the conversation.

Barnowski smiled back, then scratched his chin before resuming the story. "Henderson told folks he worked as a driller for different oil companies and took on work wherever he wanted to. Gave people the impression he could pick and choose when and where and *if* he wanted to work. The gunsmith told me Henderson usually took three or four jobs a year that kept him out of town six to eight months at a time. One year Henderson came back in a cast and using a cane. Naturally I got curious. I got the doc's autopsy report before I picked you up at the airport."

"And found out the leg hadn't been broken?"

"Oh, it was broken all right. But the doc said the fracture was caused by a bullet and not a bad fall."

"So you got curious."

Barnowski grinned. "Naturally. I took a look at the body myself. The guy was covered with scars—knives, bullets, some jagged and others tended neat. I seen scars like that before. Some of 'em I see every morning in the mirror."

Bolan nodded, understanding the deputy's words. He wore scars himself, every one of them a memory.

"So I kind of figured Henderson didn't work in the oil business at all."

"But it gave him good credibility in town and explained his comings and goings."

"Yeah, and it also explained his money. Henderson played a fast, loose life around here, which sometimes caused considerable concern in the older folks. I didn't tell the G-man about this last night. Figured if he wanted to do things the hard way, he could trip over it himself."

"I appreciate the information, Deputy."

"Man gets what he earns, way I see it."

Bolan shifted. "Speaking of seeing things, I was told someone was asking about Henderson yesterday."

"That's not verified," Barnowski said, "but I got it from a few good sources that a Vietnamese kid was asking a few questions about Henderson and was later seen driving by Henderson's house."

"A kid?"

Barnowski shrugged. "You know how it is with country folks, Belasko. They figure anybody that ain't growed full man-size is just a kid. I'm guessing that 'kid' is probably in his mid-twenties and has had some military experience."

"Because he took Henderson in the middle of the night?"

"No, because he took Henderson in the middle of the night when Henderson was waiting on him."

Bolan looked around the area again, trying to imagine what had been in Henderson's mind when he made his stand on top of the incline. Had he known who was hunting him? Or would this have been a normal reaction to anyone who had started asking questions about him? And how had Henderson's killer found the man when no one else seemed to be able to find a handle on what was going on? "You're sure about that?"

"Yeah," Barnowski replied. "You would be, too, if you'd had a chance to see it before the county mounties and the OSBI guys traipsed all over the area looking for clues."

Looking at the limited number of paths the killer had had to pick from, Bolan's estimation of his quarry's skill rose. To take a man like Henderson—a man who obviously had been dealing in death even after the war—in the dark was a big achievement.

"Impressive, huh?" Barnowski said.

"Yeah."

"The guy got lucky, though."

Bolan glanced at the big deputy, an inquisitive look on his face.

"Henderson hit him once at least. The crime scene guys found two different blood types out here. Most of the blood belonged to Henderson, but they found drops on some bushes down by the river that definitely belonged to someone else."

Bolan considered that, wondering if the wound would deter the assassin or even slow him down.

"I put out a notice to the local hospitals and to the ones within a hundred-mile radius," Barnowski said, "but I'm not holding my breath."

Bolan nodded, figuring the guy was too professional to stop for medical aid. As a Vietnamese he already stood out in small towns like this one. The guy wouldn't want to take the risk, even if it meant dying. He looked at Barnowski. "You said Henderson had a house in town?"

MITCHELL HENDERSON'S house was a gray rectangular structure comprised of small rooms just off the town's main street. The houses around it were close, making for narrow yards, but the backyard extended for more than a hundred fifty feet, marked by chain link fence. Johnson grass and flowering weeds grew in profusion on the other side of the fence, right up to the railroad tracks that cut diagonally through the heart of the town.

Town seemed too elaborate a name for Francis, Oklahoma. A handful of buildings covered a block and a half of Main Street, ending at the side street Barnowski had turned onto to get to Henderson's house.

They left the deputy's tan-and-white pickup parked in the graveled circle driveway in front of the house. Red mud had all but obliterated the Sheriff's Department decal on the side of the vehicle, but Bolan was sure the neighbors wouldn't fail to understand the significance of the light bar bolted across the top of the truck. One elderly man came out of his house as Bolan stood on Henderson's porch, waiting for Barnowski to unlock the door. The neighbor took a seat in a weathered rocking chair and tamped a fresh load into his pipe.

"The investigative teams have already been through Henderson's stuff," Barnowski said as he closed the door behind them and pocketed the key.

"Those people were looking for a murderer," Bolan said as he studied the twelve-foot-by-twelve-foot living room. "I'm looking for a trail and a connection that will take me beyond Mitchell." The sofa cushions hadn't been placed back neatly and lay askew on the sagging frame. Throw rugs covered the hardwood floor.

Bolan was examining the generous selection of books filling the shelves of a wall unit that separated the living room from the kitchen when he heard a scuffing noise from the upper floor. Raising an eyebrow at the deputy, the Executioner drew the Beretta. Barnowski cleared leather with his own .357.

Motioning for the deputy to remain on the first floor, Bolan took the stairs, carefully placing his weight on the outer edges of the steps so that he could cut his chances of making noise with a loose board.

His combat senses told him they weren't alone in the house. He let the 9 mm pistol lead the way, set on 3-round burst. His back and shoulders brushed against the plaster wall behind him, curiously devoid of any pictures. The Spartanism of the whole house reflected a transitory life that Bolan found disturbingly familiar.

The Warrior paused at the landing and listened. Turning, he saw that the big deputy had placed himself by the doorway with both hands on the grip of his Magnum. Barnowski was watching him intently.

Bolan followed the Beretta up the second flight of stairs, waiting for a repeat of the sound that would indicate a direction to him. A hallway at the top of the stairs led in both directions. The floor creaked somewhere to Bolan's left, followed by a sharp, involuntary inhalation.

He crept down the hallway without making a sound, then paused at a doorway and peered around the corner. Nothing moved.

The bedroom was devoid of furniture, holding only a few cardboard boxes that were covered with dust. A musty smell clogged Bolan's nose and almost made him sneeze. The bright afternoon sunlight streamed through two windows covered by faded curtains.

What had made Henderson cling to the house? Bolan wondered as he eased himself around the doorjamb. Memories of some other home from the past he'd been forced to give up in 1975? Yet the man had made no effort to make it a true home.

Bolan entered the room without disturbing the silence. The closet door set in one wall wavered slightly. Sliding into position beside the door, Bolan laid the Beretta across his heart, ready to drop it into instant target acquisition. Then he reached for the knob and yanked it open, grabbing immediately for the arm that struggled desperately to keep the door closed.

A woman's scream shattered the silence. The intruder fell to her knees, covering her head with her arms. "Don't shoot! Please don't shoot!"

After making sure the closet was empty, Bolan turned to his prisoner, sliding the 93-R into its shoulder rigging. The woman appeared to be in her late twenties or early thirties, with peroxide blond hair and vivid eye shadow. She wore a fringed leather jacket, a tight-fitting blouse that gapped admirably and jeans that looked like a second skin of faded denim. Bolan helped her up.

"Belasko?" Barnowski called from below.

After assuring the deputy that everything was in order, Bolan looked at the crying woman. "Who are you?"

"Billi Jo Kingsley. Look, I don't know nothin' about Mitch, okay? We just dated some, you know? That's all. We just dated some." She dabbed at the tears running down her cheeks with a nervous hand, snuffling. Her gaze kept darting to Bolan's eyes, then quickly away.

"What were you doing here?"

"Nothin'. I wasn't doin' nothin'."

Bolan heard Barnowski clumping up the stairs and watched the big deputy enter the room, still holding his .357. "Do you know her?"

The deputy nodded. "Yeah. Billi Jo Kingsley. She and Mitch had been seeing each other the past year or so. We questioned her last night because she was at the house when Henderson got killed."

"You're a cop?" the woman said, looking at Bolan.

The warrior nodded, noticing a dark, yellowing stain high up on one of the woman's cheekbones that the smeared makeup no longer concealed.

Her crying stopped, but the shivering continued. She wrapped her arms around herself. "You hurt my wrist when you yanked me out of there, damn it. You got no call to be doin' that." She massaged the wrist as if to emphasize her point.

Bolan stepped into the closet and took a penlight from his pocket.

"What the hell are you doing here, Billi Jo?" Barnowski asked as he holstered his .357.

"Nothin', Deputy. I just came back to get some of my things, is all."

"You lived here with Henderson?" Bolan asked as he shone the penlight along the plasterboard walls.

The woman brushed hair out of her eyes. "No. We had an arrangement, that's all." She stared at Bolan, no longer displaying the terror that had filled her. "Actually, mister, that's none of your business."

Bolan shifted dusty photo albums on the top shelf, giving the woman a brief glance. "If you don't live here, that makes you a trespasser."

She didn't say anything.

"Mr. Belasko's a federal agent, Billi Jo," Barnowski said.

Bolan saw some of the woman's recently acquired composure shatter and continued to move Mason jars that were stacked on the shelf. "Do you have a reason to be afraid of federal agents?"

"No."

The answer was too quick, and Bolan knew it. He paused. "But you knew Henderson was, didn't you?"

"Mitch wasn't afraid of nobody," she said stubbornly.

"He's dead," Bolan told her in a harsh voice. "Maybe he should have been. Maybe you should be, too."

She bit her lower lip.

"Did Henderson tell you about the people looking for him?" Bolan asked.

"No."

"But he knew about the Vietnamese guy who'd been asking questions about him?"

"Yes. Everybody in town knew about him."

"Why didn't Henderson go to the police?" Bolan removed the boxes of jars, placing them gently on the floor outside the closet.

"He didn't want to. He said it was something he could take care of himself."

"Did himself a hell of a job now, too, didn't he, Billi Jo?" Barnowski said.

"Where did you get the bruise on your face?" Bolan asked.

The woman touched her cheek unconsciously. "Mitch. Sometimes he'd get mad, drunk. Sometimes he liked to hit."

Bolan ran the penlight's beam over the plasterboard walls above the closet shelf. One side was conspicuously clear of spiderwebs. He pushed tentatively and felt it give under his fingertips. A flood of warm air wrapped around his hand.

"Hey," the woman said suddenly. "Hey, you got no business in there."

The light from the penlight bounced off the side of a fireproof strongbox. Bolan reached inside the cavity and pulled the box out, finding it surprisingly heavy. "Was this what you were looking for?" he asked as he carried the strongbox to the center of the room. Taking a lock pick kit from inside his jacket, he released the catch and lifted the lid. The box was filled with gold coins.

Barnowski whistled sharply.

"You got no right to that, mister," the woman said forcefully.

Bolan removed one of the gold coins and examined it—a Krugerrand, minted last year. Now he had a direction to give to Brognola and Kurtzman. Krugerrands had been removed from the American market a few years back. For Henderson to have any of them in his possession meant the man probably had been in South Africa. For the man to have left them here instead of taking them with him meant that he had expected no trouble dealing with the Vietnamese. It also meant he'd expected the one man to be the end of the search. Why? Because the CIA hadn't been the ones to penetrate the ID he had set up? Assuming he'd been able to handle the man stalking him, Henderson hadn't been expecting to have to continue running.

Bolan closed his fingers over the heaviness of the gold, feeling more than its weight in his palm. Fifteen years of running and hiding; fifteen years of sharpening skills developed in the jungles of Vietnam in whatever special operations the CIA had put together all those years ago. What kind of men was he tracking? Scared and skilled, yeah. You never found an enemy more dangerous than the guy who knew how to control his own fear and use it against you. And what would they do now that they realized their covers had been blown?

Run and hide? No doubt. But they would strike back, too. Just to keep things interesting.

Bolan dropped the coin back into the box, feeling now more than ever that he was sitting on a powder keg. He relocked it and handed it to Barnowski.

"Hey," the woman said again. "You ain't got no right to that, Deputy."

"It's evidence," Barnowski replied tiredly. "We'll let the courts decide."

Bolan led the way down the stairs, turning everything over in his mind, trying to decide what he would do if he was in Major Shane Innis's shoes. React, sure as hell. But how? He needed to know more about the man, about the circumstances Innis had found himself in at the end of the war. Why had something like Mad Dog been put into effect by the CIA? The questions turned in on themselves, dovetailing into more questions.

Flickering movement caught his attention as they walked toward the door. He paused to lift a curtain, combat senses flooding him with the need to move. A green late-sixties Mustang had pulled to a stop in the middle of the street. Two men sat inside it, studying the pickup. Bolan held up a hand to stop Barnowski.

"What's up?" the deputy asked.

"We've got company," Bolan said as he drew the Beretta. "Take her out the back way."

Gripping the woman by the elbow, Barnowski hustled her toward the back of the house.

One of the men in the sports car got out and unlocked the trunk. Bolan immediately recognized the tubular shape that came away in the man's hands as a LAW 80. Before the guy had a chance to aim, the Executioner smashed out the window with the flat of his hand and brought up his Beretta.

His target dropped to the ground, and Bolan directed the 93-R's muzzle toward the driver. The window shattered a second after the driver disappeared. The Warrior squeezed the trigger and emptied the Beretta's clip, firing to give the deputy time to get out of the house with the woman.

Bolan recharged his weapon and rolled around the corner of the window to glance at the back of the house. Barnowski was nowhere in sight. When he turned back around, the driver had a mini-Uzi wrapped in his fist. The staccato burst of the weapon ripped through the window, tearing at the curtain and punching wooden chips from the windowframe.

Knowing the man with the LAW wouldn't hesitate now, the Executioner ran toward the back of the house, hoping the deputy had gotten clear. He bounced off the doorjamb that opened up to the tiny kitchen, and threw himself over the threshold. He hit the screen door, tearing it from its hinges, then the explosion's concussion sent him spinning to the ground.

For a moment Mack Bolan was lost between heartbeats, riding out the concussive force of the explosion behind him and waiting for the sudden impact of the ground. The yard was a blur of green beneath him, and his senses were overloaded with what was happening to him. Then his reflexes took over, tucking his body into a shoulder roll that managed to control his headlong eruption of movement.

He stood shakily, his hand locked around the Beretta. Sweeping the backyard as he brought the 9 mm up to the ready position, Bolan found the deputy covering the woman with his body. "Barnowski?"

The deputy stirred and rolled off the woman. The .357 was in one fist as he recovered his Stetson with the other. "I'm fine. How many did you count?"

"Two, in a green Mustang. I don't know how they're set for armament." Bolan moved forward to the left side of the house. The structure appeared to be listing badly to one side, as if a sudden breeze might topple it. Smoke curled from the incendiary scattered inside the shattered living room.

"I'd say they're armed pretty fucking good," Barnowski said sourly as he took up position on the other side of the house.

Bolan followed the Beretta's lead, knowing if he didn't take out the gunners fast there would be innocent blood spilled around the hellzone. He paused at the side of the house, listening to the tentative footsteps made by someone on the wooden porch. Then something impacted on the front door, followed by a muffled curse.

The Executioner flattened himself against the house and swung around the corner, letting his weapon chart his course, watching the man on the porch swing blue eyes widened with fear and surprise toward him. The silenced Beretta chugged softly in the Executioner's fist and blew out the frightened lights in the man's glance. The Uzi in the attacker's arms uttered a short burst that ripped splinters from the porch. The chatter died away seconds after the gunner did.

The lawn in front of Bolan erupted in an unexpected zigzag dance that echoed the familiar stutter of an Ingram submachine gun.

Rather than get pinned by the fire, Bolan threw himself away from the house and over the chain link fence separating the lots. He rolled and came up in a kneeling position, placing a 3-round burst across the Mustang's windshield that blasted the rearview mirror into a crazy spin.

The hollow boom of Barnowski's .357 echoed between the houses in rapid double action. Bolan watched the deputy break free of the protection afforded by Henderson's wrecked home to take up refuge behind his pickup.

Gunfire rattled from a new direction, chopping into a mimosa sapling in the middle of the yard and sending the miniature branches flying through the air like confetti. Bolan trained the 93-R on the cream-colored coupe highballing down the street into the battleground. He counted two men in that vehicle as he stood and provided covering fire for the deputy.

At least one of the enemy rounds hit Barnowski, sending the man into an off-balance spiral that landed him beside the pickup. He scrambled for cover, dragging a leg behind him.

Bolan stepped outside of himself for a moment, focusing on his target, keeping the Beretta pumping, chugging parabellums through the windshield, seeking the driver. The coupe veered suddenly, pulling left to careen through a yard across the street. A ceramic birdbath shattered into fragments when it impacted against the car's grille.

Bolan dropped the empty magazine and reloaded on the run as the Mustang's driver pursued him with the Ingram. The warrior hurled himself into the drainage ditch beside the road as the .45-caliber slugs slashed the air above his head. He peered over the edge of the ditch, scrambling on elbows and knees now, feeling the sharp bite of a stone on one knee. He ignored it, tracking with the Beretta as the passenger in the coupe opened the driver's door and shoved the corpse out. Reluctant to chance shooting into the house the vehicle was stalled in front of, Bolan waited.

Behind him, Barnowski had forced himself to a sprawling stand against the pickup. Bolan watched as the deputy popped open the door and reached under the pickup's seat, dragging an M-14 into view.

The Ingram wielded by the hitter in the Mustang chewed through the pickup's windows, showering Barnowski with glass, and exploded the light bar on the cab. Then the deputy moved to the back of his vehicle, lifting the M-14 with an easy familiarity. Before the Mustang's driver could track onto his new position, Barnowski's stream of tumblers dissolved the man's features in a sudden crimson eruption.

The coupe reversed out of the yard, its tires slipping and screaming for traction. Before the driver could pull his machine into a forward gear, Bolan was out of the ditch, tracking with the Beretta. The windshield cracked from a central spot outward, like the circles on the surface of a pond. The vehicle continued backward without guidance, finally slamming into a huge pecan tree. The tires rotated for a moment, then the engine died.

Bolan rammed another magazine home, replacing the one he'd fired dry. The silence was intense now that the sound of the gunplay had faded. Holding the Beretta in an upright position as he walked down the road, Bolan scanned the vehicles for signs of life, aware that Barnowski was backing his play from the pickup with the M-14.

All of the men were dead, and none had any identification in their possession. The features of only two of the gunners would be useful in trying to identify them later.

Bolan leathered the Beretta after he checked the last body. The attack force had been equipped with heavy armament, ordnance a man couldn't get unless he was connected to an arms dealer. The gunners didn't appear to be CIA, either, which meant someone else was cutting into the action or more of the mystery guys had turned up. He wouldn't know until their fingertips were run through the computers.

He turned and walked back to Barnowski. Crimson stained the deputy's left thigh, but there was a sardonic grin on his face. "How bad's the leg?" Bolan asked.

"Doesn't hurt," Barnowski said as he extended his lighter. "Yet. If I'm lucky, I'll get to do a little fishing the next few days. If not, I'll be catching calls at the office and giving good telephone. I've got a slave driver for a boss." He slipped the bandanna off his head to tie around his leg, wincing with the effort. "The cavalry should be here in about thirty minutes." He let down the tailgate on the pickup and sat on it.

Bolan nodded. "I've got a plane waiting at the airport. Are you going to be all right?"

"Except for all the paperwork the sheriff's going to want out of me, I'm fine."

The warrior removed a notepad and pen from his jacket pocket, tore off a sheet of paper and wrote down Brognola's telephone number. "If somebody gets a line on the names of any of these people, call this number and leave a message for me."

Barnowski pocketed the notepaper. "I'll take care of it myself. You're into some serious shit here, man, and I don't want to take the chance of one of the other guys putting this on a back burner and forgetting about it."

"I appreciate it," Bolan replied, shaking the man's hand. "Take care of yourself." He moved toward the coupe and pulled the body from behind the steering wheel. The engine caught on the first turn of the ignition, and he pulled back onto the road, watching the living and the dead fade away in his rearview mirror.

ANTICIPATION FILLED Innis, demanding blood. Sometimes the waiting was worth it, he thought as he peered through the window of the hotel room he'd broken into. The impatience, as long as he made sure it stayed controlled, added a knife edge to the hunger that gnawed within him.

Hacker had never understood the hunger that filled Innis and refused to be satiated, but Hacker had used it and allowed it to feed on whoever the CIA had wanted terminated—as long as the terminations had been geared to escalating American involvement in the war. Hacker had even overstepped his authority at times by issuing Judson orders that Innis was to be given a creative hand in the assassinations—the more grisly the better.

In one instance the suggestion had resulted in the mutilation-execution of a South Vietnamese diplomat's wife in Saigon. The murder had never reached the American newspapers in the States, but had found its way to the ears of visiting American war lobbyists who had pushed Congress to give more aid to the South Vietnamese government in 1965.

Hacker's only real mistake was in believing something like Mad Dog would have rectified the situation the Agency had been responsible for. Hacker had been convinced the free hand the team had been given during the war had somehow tainted Innis. Judson had told Innis that.

Innis smiled at the memory as he kept watch over the hotel across the street. Hacker hadn't known that same blood lust had been a motivating factor during most of Innis's life. The freedom he'd gotten from the CIA hadn't created anything, only given it room to mature and reach for new horizons.

Night covered the downtown section of Luanda. Little more than fourteen hours had passed since the attack on Innis's yacht. He'd spent the time assembling his forces, getting word to Judson and the rest of the Hawks, preparing to strike back at the person or persons stalking them. He'd also used his local intel sources to find out that the CIA men Hacker had assigned to take care of the loose end in Angola were staying in the hotel across the street.

Innis moved quietly in the darkness. Then, with only an infrequent glance, he opened the briefcase he'd carried into the room and assembled the weapon that lay in the form-fit interior. The rifle was a duplicate of a Goncz Laser Carbine he'd used on specific take-out missions in Angola and Namibia with good results. The laser could pinpoint a target up to four hundred yards away. The door to the hotel wasn't even half that.

Judson had told him Hacker had disappeared some years after the war, lost in the same bureaucratic red tape that had misplaced the files on the Hawks and Mad Dog. But Innis had never once fooled himself into believing that Hacker was dead. Slipped between the cracks of changing politics into a new identity that didn't have the taint of the Vietnam War lingering on it—that Innis could believe. He'd somehow always felt sure he would know when the man died, as if they were connected by some intangible umbilical cord that had grown during the formation of the team. Judson had been a tool, as surely under Innis's charismatic control today as he had been over twenty years ago. Hacker had sensed the true nature of Judson's relationship with his major. Innis knew that. Just as he knew the CIA control was content with the state of affairs as long as the missions were carried out successfully.

With nimble fingers he screwed the stock into place, then glanced at his watch. According to Innis's sources, the CIA agents would be leaving the hotel soon to catch their plane back to Japan where they would miraculously become Air Force men on leave back to Virginia.

His finger caressed the Goncz's trigger, spraying a pinpoint of ruby light against one of the unlit room's walls as he tested the laser sighting. Satisfied, he loaded the weapon and waited.

Since the attack on the yacht had been a failure, Innis chose to take it as a message from Hacker. The Goncz was going to help him leave a reply.

Once he had the rifle ready, he pressed the sliding window open and braced himself. He let out a slow breath as he counted windows to the seventh floor of the hotel opposite him, then counted three windows to the right, centering on the room his informants had told him belonged to the CIA team leader.

Thirteen minutes later the soft yellow square of light framing the room's window blinked out. Innis felt the anticipation pluck a responsive chord inside him as he let the rifle muzzle drift to street level again. His own room was three floors up, giving him a wide view of the almost deserted street and allowing him quick access to the alleys behind the building. He had his car waiting there to take him to the private jet he'd hired.

A cab, summoned by a doorman in a maroon uniform, stopped in front of the hotel. Innis shot the first two men out of the building through the head, tagging a third in the chest to send him crashing to the pavement. He also managed to hit the fourth man as he dived back into the hotel. Not bothering with the fifth man, who had disappeared along with his wounded companion, Innis shifted his sights to the cabdriver. A bullet through the driver's neck as he tried to pull away sent the car lurching out of control and into the path of traffic. A flatbed truck hit the vehicle, and the force of the impact spun it around.

Innis tossed the Goncz onto the bed and let himself out of the room as the noise level on the street rose dramatically. He trotted to the fire escape, breathing easily, knowing the force inside him wasn't satisfied with the relatively minor havoc he'd wreaked. Knowing, too, that it was only the beginning until he got the unit together again and they made one last mission across familiar enemy ground.

Message received, Hacker, Innis thought grimly as he double-timed it down the stairs. RSVP attached.

MACK BOLAN SHIFTED uneasily behind the desk in Hal Brognola's Washington, D.C. office. Every fiber of his warrior's being cried out to be on the move, doing something, but the strategist in him realized the need for more intel.

Sighing tiredly, he levered himself out of the swivel chair and made his way to the coffee maker. He poured himself another cup and leaned against the wall as he sipped at the brew.

It was damn hard trying to hit something you couldn't see and only had the vaguest of feelings about. He was chasing the ghost of a trail fifteen years dead.

The whole question was like an old wound that wasn't quite healed. At the center was a sore that had festered unseen until it had suddenly broken open again.

An old wound, but who did it belong to? The CIA? To a degree, sure. Its involvement was unimpeachable. But the Company hadn't initiated the confrontation. Neither had the men who had turned up dead. If they were once all part of a secret group that had maintained a degree of communication over the years, as the Manchester-South African gold connection indicated, they evidently had an operation going on for some time. They wouldn't have wanted to call attention to themselves even if they had had some sort of falling-out.

Then there was the joker in the deck: the unidentified Vietnamese who had killed Henderson in Oklahoma. Brognola was supposed to be gathering the coroner's information from that state now to match it against the 9 mm slugs taken from Lawrence's body in L.A.

Bolan was willing to believe the bullets would match.

He slipped a thumb inside the Beretta's shoulder harness absently, shifting the familiar weight to a new position. Returning to the desk covered with the hard-copy intel Brognola had managed to get his hands on, Bolan checked the contents against his mental file. All three of the men had past histories that were represented in the documentation: birth certificates, high school diplomas, Social Security and income tax reports. But those histories ended in 1962 for Henderson and Lawrence, and in 1964 for Stoddard, sucked away by a black hole created by an unknown party in the CIA.

Both of the other murdered men had possessed recent battle scars as had Henderson. Meaning what? That they'd been involved with Manchester in mercenary work? The conclusion seemed logical.

Bolan riffled through the sheets until he got to the slim report covering the activities of one Timothy Lancaster Manchester. According to the files Kurtzman had been able to dig up by referencing data bases of the different alphabet agencies, Manchester was a known mercenary major operating in the African theater about whom little was known.

Major Shane Innis remained as much of an enigma as the true identities of the three murdered men. Ditto for Hacker.

Taking the blurred photograph of Manchester from the file, Bolan leaned it against the adjustable lamp clipped to the desk. The guy could have been anywhere from his early forties to mid-fifties. His hair was slicked back, and the black-and-white picture didn't allow Bolan to guess what the hair color was. The man was big-boned without being beefy, with harsh features that almost seemed cruel.

Bolan held his coffee cup in both hands and stared into the colorless eyes of the photograph, trying to imagine what the guy might have looked like fifteen years earlier, wondering what Innis had looked like.

Leaning forward, he scooped up the phone and dialed the Stony Man number and Aaron Kurtzman's extension, knowing the technology involved between the two points never allowed the call to be traced to the Farm, deep in the Blue Ridge Mountains of Virginia. Brognola had swept the CIA bugs from his office earlier in the day.

"Kurtzman," the Bear answered in his booming voice.

Bolan shifted back in the swivel chair, still staring at the photograph. Had Quot been telling the truth when he said Innis and Manchester were the same man? "Aaron, it's me."

"Striker! As last I get to talk to the guy who's been tying up my computer time with answerless questions."

"Maybe I've got one you can answer this time, big guy."

"Shoot."

Dead man's eyes, Bolan thought as he kept his mind focused on Manchester. "Have you still got a copy of the Manchester file you sent over?"

"Affirmative."

"Are you familiar with the computer-enhanced aging process the National Center for Missing and Exploited Children is using to help find missing children?"

"Yeah. I've talked with Barrows and Sadler, the people who wrote the program. It's not completely foolproof, but in most cases it helps produce a reasonably current picture of what the missing child might look like. At least it's better than using a picture of a three-year-old to search for a child who's now seven or eight. They've been pretty successful with it."

"Can you tap into the system?"

"Better than that. I've got the program built into the systems I use. Have you got somebody you want aged?"

Bolan grinned. "No, actually, I've got somebody I want to make young again."

"Manchester?"

"Yeah. Think you can manage?"

"Give me a minute. The program hasn't been designed to run backward, but I should be able to loop it and come up with something."

Bolan waited, listening as Kurtzman tapped computer keys at the other end of the line. If the Bear said it couldn't be done, Bolan would believe it. Computers were Kurtzman's weapons in the war against the savages.

"How many years do you want me to take off this guy, Striker?"

"Start with twenty years."

"One Fountain of Youth coming up," Kurtzman said. "Got it?"

"Yeah. Grecian Gray ain't got nothing on this program. What do you want me to do with it?"

"Run it back through the ID."

"Under the Manchester name or the Innis name?"

Bolan stroked his chin. "Neither. Run it through cold, just the facial."

"Damn!"

"What's wrong?"

"I see where you're headed now, Striker. I should have thought of this."

Professionalism. Bolan could hear it in the big man's words. And pride. "Don't sweat it, Aaron. Hal and I have had you tracking names and intel for the past two days. Sometimes it takes an outside perspective to line up new thinking."

"Yeah, well, maybe one of these days I'll catch you trying to screw a silencer onto a revolver the way they do on television and we'll be even."

Bolan grinned.

"I'm in. So far, so good. We're scanning through FBI files now. There. I've routed it into the CIA. Give yourself a cigar, Striker. We've got a tie-in to the name."

"The program dead-ended in the CIA files?"

"Yep. The same place as the others did. So now what have you got?"

Bolan leaned forward, staring at the photograph intently. "A face, Aaron, and that's more than I had to work with before. Thanks." He broke the connection. He had another piece of the puzzle, or at least a name for it, but he still had no way to fit the Vietnamese shooter into the situation.

Or maybe the shooter didn't fit.

Bolan examined the possibility in a new light. Everything that had happened so far had seemed to be the result of trying to take care of the unexpected. The only thing about the whole operation that appeared to be premeditated was the murders themselves.

But that chain of events was impossible to follow, too. Since three of the unknown number of whatever team the CIA had made Innis responsible for had been killed—presumably by the same guy—it stood to reason that the motivation for the murders was somewhere in the past the Agency was determined to keep under lock and key.

Which made Major Shane Innis the only live variable still in the game, as far as Bolan knew.

Footsteps whispered through the hall as shoes hit the carpet. Two minutes later Hal Brognola strode into the room with an angry look on his face and an unlit cigar clamped between his teeth. He glanced at the photograph on the desk and scowled. "Manchester?"

Bolan shook his head. "Major Shane Innis, late of the United States Army."

"You got it verified?"

"Aaron did."

"Terrific." Brognola spit the mangled remains of the cigar into the trash bin beside the desk. "I've got a news update on Innis for you."

Bolan waited.

"Apparently a hard crew with orders from an unspecified source in Langley tried to whack Innis in Angola earlier. As a result, the State Department is burning the midnight oil tonight trying to figure out a nice way to recover four bodies, a hospital patient and a man who was taken into custody fleeing the scene of a massacre, all of whom were American agents operating in the country under falsified papers."

"What about Innis?"

"He hasn't turned up under his own or the Manchester name. Yet."

"He won't, Hal. The Agency might have flushed him out of hiding, but they haven't put him away. This guy's on the move, and he's running for his life. Bet on it."

Sluggish, Whit Talbot struggled against the recliner until he could sit up enough to reach the telephone hanging on the wall to his right. He blinked against the room's darkness as he dragged the receiver to his ear, finally realizing there was nothing wrong with his vision. The living room of the spacious apartment he shared with Mandy was empty, and he wondered when she had gone to bed. He glanced at the clock—1:00 a.m.

"Talbot," he said hoarsely into the mouthpiece.

"I was told you left a message for me to call you back."

The homicide detective recognized the graveyard voice at once. "Right. Hang on." Talbot reached back toward the wall and switched on the small reading lamp beside the recliner. He pulled a legal pad from the side pocket of the chair. "I hope you have a few extra minutes because I've got to make a couple of presentations here, then tie them together. I promise I can make it worth your time."

"Okay."

"CIA agents arrived in town a couple of hours after the scene with Quot, with enough federal paper behind them to liberate the prisoner I'd taken and the body of the man you killed to save me. They didn't say thank you, excuse me or even try to provide any reason why the men would attempt to shoot me down in the street or explain why they assassinated Quot. I called a friend of mine and had him do some digging on Quot, only to have my friend call me back to say the reaction he'd gotten to his questions was based on some kind of paranoia at the Agency. Some of the background on Quot that I did get my hands on indicated the man had once been connected with the CIA during the war. Remembering the War Memorial killings the newspapers have been full of lately, I followed a gut feeling. You ever play hunches, Agent Belasko?"

"All the time."

"Yeah, that's what I figured. You don't act like the type to wait until all the cards are on the table. I also figured Quot was a hunch that almost paid off for you. That's why the CIA guys weren't all over him when you blew into town. I say almost because I'm still able to get in touch with you. If your assignment had been completed, I have the feeling you would have vanished by now. My friend said you were something of a mystery yourself. The last time he remembered your name in the media was during the attempted assassination of the President and Gorbachev, and you were listed as some kind of high-priced security talent. Not a member of the Justice Department."

Talbot made himself relax in the chair and glance over his notes, refreshing himself on the information. Normally his handwriting was neat and his thoughts organized. Now the scribble looked pained and ran all over the pages. He wished he had a cup of coffee. "Assuming you weren't in San Francisco just to investigate the crack operation Quot was operating, I guessed you were looking for the man behind the War Memorial murders. According to an unidentified source in the *Washington Post*, the War Memorial people who were killed were at one time attached to the CIA liaison in Vietnam. So now I had the

CIA connected to the War Memorial killings, to Quot and to you, because you guys obviously don't work together."

"If you're asking me to verify any of this, Sergeant, I can't."

"I know. I'm not asking you to. This is just to let you know how my mind's been working. If I make any quantum leaps that take me completely out in left field, let me know and I'll save us both some time by hanging up."

"Let's hear what you have."

"Okay. That's the end of act one. Curtain goes up on act two. I have in my possession, thanks to you, certain documents that hold crippling knowledge of Carmine DiCarlo's drug empire. I wanted to test them. So I pulled in a young dealer named Leon Farber who works the gay area and did a prelim investigation. I chose Farber because he's still a virgin when it comes to the state's penal institution. He's never been busted for anything worse than a traffic fine. I leaned on him, told him how much the big, strong prisoners loved the young stuff in the cage and how I could hold him for twenty-four hours in lockup before I hit him with any charges. He started spilling his guts, naming names, giving dates, times and places. While I'm taking this down, adding to what you've already given me, he tells me about a drug buy that went sour about seven months ago. It stirred up some animosity between DiCarlo and Tiep before they got things worked out. It seems a young Vietnamese male who had been in Tiep's employ took down the drug buyers and made off with eighty-five to ninety thousand dollars. DiCarlo wasn't too upset because the money didn't belong to him. The smash-and-grab guy hadn't been interested in the five keys of crack at all. Only the money. How do you like it so far?"

"You're a persistent man, Sergeant, but where are you headed with this?"

"It gets better, Belasko. During the money snatch, the Vietnamese guy had to blast one of the money men in self-defense with an Uzi. I looked up the case and pulled the files for the ballistics reports. Then, I had L.A. fax me a copy of the ballistics reports on the man who was killed there. Guess what?"

"The bullets matched."

"Brass ring on your first try."

"Why are you coming to me with this?"

"Because I can't go any farther with it. L.A.'s out of my jurisdiction and I got pulled off active duty until the shooting board clears me. Standard procedure, true, but I think the spook brigade had something to do with it, too. Before they were able to take their corpse away, I lifted his prints and ran them through the computer. Got a big Access Denied for my trouble and the chief yelling in my ear less than thirty minutes after that, telling me the CIA people were off-limits."

"Who knows the ballistics match?"

"You," Talbot said, "and me."

"Do you have a name for the Vietnamese?"

"I talked to Tiep at the safehouse. He's still there, by the way. I figure if I bring him in right now, somebody might decide he knew almost as much as Quot and decide to waste him, too."

"Tiep doesn't know anything about the War Memorial murders."

"That's what he told me, too. Problem is, you and I might believe him, but the other 'good' guys on the scene aren't exactly pursuing this in a logical fashion. But Tiep did know the name. Khoi." Talbot spelled it. "He also told me Khoi is a little on the strange side. Quot brought him in from the Vietnam end of the operation almost a year ago. According to Tiep, Khoi is very good with the language and with weapons. He's also into some kind of Zen philosophy and kept to himself the whole time he worked for Quot." He paused. "I suppose you've heard about the War Memorial killing in Oklahoma."

Bolan said yes.

"The news sources also indicated a Vietnamese male is being hunted for questioning. By the time I'd heard that, I wasn't surprised anymore."

"You do good work, Sergeant."

"Yeah, well, I've carried the ball as far as I can at this end. I also happen to have a spare set of the prints I took from the CIA corpse if you think you can do anything with it."

"It won't help my operation any," Bolan admitted, "but it may serve to leverage a little breathing space from the CIA." He gave the Justice Department's Pennsylvania address and asked that the package be marked care of Hal Brognola.

"One other thing. Tiep said Khoi had a scar on his chest, a big thing that looked like it had been carved by a butcher knife. Not a lot of Quot's people knew it was there, but Tiep saw it a couple of times. He said it looked like some kind of hawk."

"A hawk?"

There was no mistaking the interest in the cold voice.

"Yeah. Ring any bells?"

"Maybe."

Irritation flared inside Talbot, but he brushed it aside. No matter how far he carried his investigation, there were still going to be loose ends as far as he was concerned. Belasko was operating strictly on a need-to-know basis and the homicide detective couldn't blame him. It would have been hard enough trying to piece together events of something that happened all those years ago in another country without having CIA death troops knocking on your door, as well.

"I appreciate your time, Sergeant."

"Oh, this isn't free, Agent Belasko. Sometime when this is over, I want the two of us to have a quiet drink somewhere and have you give me the grand tour on this thing."

"If I can."

"Fair enough."

Bolan broke the connection.

Talbot hung up the phone, surprised at the sense of satisfaction he'd received from the conversation. He didn't doubt that the information he'd given the Justice man was valuable in some aspects, perhaps not necessary, but worthwhile just the same. It felt good knowing that he had carried it as far as he could, and almost felt that good knowing that Belasko was in a position to stretch it even farther.

He levered himself out of the recliner, pausing to work out painful twinges from kinked muscles, then padded in sock feet to the bedroom to wake Mandy. She was one of the few women he knew who could get up out of bed in the middle of the night when he was feeling restless and go eat Mexican food. And you didn't find that many young, beautiful women with an intelligence you could respect who would listen to an old homicide cop at two o'clock in the morning, then share their bed with the guy later. He warmed at the thought, feeling only a little guilty when he thought of Belasko.

KHOI DROVE through Miami with remembered ease, blending in with the traffic moving away from the beaches toward the city's downtown area. Rock and roll spilled out of the Camaro's four speakers, and for a moment he was swept back in time to the months he had spent working in the area.

The long days of backbreaking labor swamping out yachts and fishing boats had helped him keep his impatience curbed until he'd found a way to gain the trust of Drew Judson. And the work had kept him in shape as well as providing him with contacts among the smugglers and gunrunners.

He paused at a traffic light, listening to the music, temporarily amazed at how far his quest had taken him from home. Then disgust filled him. Home? He had known no home since his mother had died.

His fingers tightened on the steering wheel as he gazed out over the bright lights clinging to buildings on both sides of the street. The wound in his leg twinged, and he reached for the vial of antibiotics that had been only one of his purchases from the black marketeer he'd met tonight. He shook three of the penicillin tablets onto his palm, tossed them into his mouth and chewed them thoroughly before swallowing.

The traffic started forward again, and he followed mechanically. Infection had already started to set into the wound despite his attempts to keep it clean. He had used a knife earlier, in the motel room he had rented, to open it and let small runnels of pus out. He had felt relief immediately. Still, a fever had developed and now covered him with a fine sheen of perspiration.

Hopefully the antibiotic would take effect soon, or at least delay the majority of the infection and keep it at a level he could deal with. There was still much to do.

Smiley had told him there were twelve men in the group he hunted. Drew Judson had retained files on five of them in his possession, at least five that Khoi had found. Perhaps there were more, secreted in other places of Judson's massive house, but the five were all he needed to get started on his hunt. Even having the new names of the others would have been of no use at this point. They were all moving now, meeting their master, Innis, to decide what to do.

Khoi knew the men would have no choice. The CIA was looking for them now and, from the events he had witnessed so far, the Agency wouldn't stop until Innis and his group were finally laid to rest. Khoi's deliberate naming of them had left them nowhere to run except Cambodia.

He felt better as he turned into a residential section of the city, cruising silently now, letting his thoughts collect. Innis's resources would be unavailable to him now, as would the financial resources of the other men. Their secrets, their loyalties would pull them together. Alone they would surely die. They knew that. Only together could they even attempt to seize a chance at a new life from Cambodia, a country still racked by war.

Khoi drove past Drew Judson's house, a large, rambling relic native to the area. Construction teams had installed the latest heating and cooling systems inside the structure only a few years ago, after Judson's retirement, and they had added an expensive security system that protected the grounds. Other than that, the two-story mansion hadn't been touched except for occasional restorative work.

Khoi had worked on the estate until a month ago when he'd started tracing his first victim. He'd feel bad about having to destroy Judson's home, if it came to that. During the time he'd worked for the man, Judson had been fair-minded, friendly and eager to talk to anyone who would listen. Oddly Judson seemed to be the closest thing to a friend that Khoi had since coming to the United States, yet the man had also been in charge of Innis. It was hard to imagine the crippled old man even associating with someone like Major Shane Innis or taking part in the atrocities the unit had committed in the name of war.

Yet Smiley had been sure of that. The CIA had cut the orders for the group and Captain Drew Judson had been the military liaison for the operations.

For now, Khoi felt compassion for the old man. Innis had carried out the missions he'd been given, but it was he who had chosen the manner in which they were to be carried out. Not Judson. It had been war, Khoi knew that. Both sides in the war had been guilty of brutality. Khoi knew that, as well. It hadn't been the war that had brought him this far, though. It had been just one small piece of it, and it made him angrier when he realized that Innis would probably never even remember the episode.

He readjusted the Glock-19 in its shoulder holster under his windbreaker, wishing he had time to test the weapon he'd purchased only hours ago. The Uzi was in the trunk of the Camaro with the rest of the ordnance he'd bought on the black market. It had taken most of his remaining money to buy the weapons and hire a pilot who was familiar enough with Cambodia to airdrop him in.

Since Khoi had drawn attention to Innis again after all these years, and since the CIA had its own files with a Judson connection, Miami was rapidly becoming a hot spot. The United States was hostile territory to them both, and he knew Innis had realized that. If it hadn't been for the secret that still lay buried somewhere within Cambodia's borders, there would have been no telling where Innis might have guided the Hawks, or if he would have guided them at all. In all probability Innis would have abandoned them to their own fates if he hadn't needed them. But need them he did, and Khoi planned to hasten their departure with a pointed nudge.

MACK BOLAN MADE the tail less than five minutes out of the Justice Department parking area. Night still covered Pennsylvania Avenue, but traffic was already picking up as the early risers started filing in from the suburbs for another workday.

The red Jeep Cherokee Brognola had arranged for his use was a definite liability under the circumstances. Taking a right, Bolan turned into Fourteenth Street, angling away from the meeting place Greg Bowen had arranged over the phone. The dark blue sedan stayed with him, changing to an alternate lane of traffic this time.

Bowen hadn't been specific about the subject of the meet, but Bolan knew through Brognola's contacts that the CIA section chief had been placed in charge of the War Memorial murders. Bowen had been an ally recently, though an unwilling one at first; but when the chips were down, the man had backed Bolan's play to take out an assassin code-named Ice Wolf.

Bowen had tried to keep the worry out of his voice during the telephone conversation, but Bolan had been aware of the effort it had taken him to keep his tone light.

Bolan watched as the sedan became gradually ensnared in the increasing morning traffic. The Warrior paced the Cherokee, made sure he caught the red light at the H Street junction and came to a stop. He glanced at the sedan, now directly in behind him, then stepped out of the vehicle in one fluid motion, clearing the Beretta from its leather as he moved back toward the tail.

Morning wind whipped over him as he let the guy see the 9 mm clenched in both fists. The man started to reach for something under the dashboard, but two rounds from the silenced 93-R through the passenger side of the windshield froze him in place.

Aware of the startled glances of the other motorists, Bolan stopped at the front of the sedan. "Out of the car," he ordered.

The man started to say something, then looked at the holes in his windshield and thought better of it. Keeping one hand on his head, he opened the sedan door and eased himself out. "You don't know what you're doing," the man warned as he stood beside his car.

Traffic moved on beside them as the light turned green and car horns honked impatiently behind the sedan. "Down on your face, hands locked behind your head," Bolan ordered.

Grumbling, the man followed directions. With the barrel of the 9 mm boring into the side of his prisoner's face, Bolan knelt and lifted the man's coat and removed a Detonics .45 Combat Master Mark VI from a hip holster. He pocketed the pistol and used the man's own handcuffs to secure his hands behind his back. Taking the man's wallet from inside the jacket, Bolan flipped it open long enough to check the ID, not surprised to find out the man was with the Central Intelligence Agency. Brognola had been successful in flushing the bugs out of his office, but he couldn't keep the watchdogs away.

"You're not going to get away with this, Belasko," the young agent said.

"Get away with what?" Bolan asked as he reached inside the sedan. He yanked a handful of wires out of the back of the shortwave radio mounted on the floor, then broke the ignition key off in the switch and pocketed the key ring after making sure it held the handcuff key.

"This is bullshit, Belasko," the agent snarled as he tried to slop around on the street.

"I agree. But you guys are the ones who made the rules. Don't start bitching now if the game gets a little rough."

Bolan knelt and used the radio's microphone cord to bind the agent's ankles. When he finished he stood and looked down at the man. "When you report back to whoever sent you on this little excursion, tell him I'm not going to back off until I get some answers, and I don't give a damn how many people I have to go through to get them."

Spotting an empty cab stopped by the traffic light and knowing he couldn't take the Cherokee anywhere, Bolan jogged over to it and flashed his Justice ID at the driver. He climbed into the back just as a police siren started knifing through the din created by the outraged motorists.

He watched the scene fade away through the rear window as he gave the cabbie an address on New York Avenue, hoping that the tail had been designed for him and not alerted by the call Greg Bowen had made.

"I'D CONVINCED MYSELF you weren't coming," Bowen said as Bolan took a seat at the table at the back of the crowded café.

"I had some company along the way," Bolan said.

The CIA section chief looked tired and haggard, squinting bloodshot eyes against the curling smoke of his cigarette. "We're talking Company company?"

"Yeah."

Bowen cursed, running a hand along his stubbled jaw. He smashed out his cigarette in the overflowing ashtray, watching the action intently. "I guess you know I'm supposed to be in charge of the CIA end of this investigation."

Bolan nodded. Their conversation died for a moment as a young waitress with bags under her eyes poured Bolan a cup of coffee and refilled Bowen's cup.

"I guess you've also been able to figure out that I don't know exactly everything that's going on around me."

Bolan nodded once again, sensing the ragged edge that lay just under the thin veneer of composure Bowen was stubbornly clinging to.

"I didn't even know you were connected with this thing until a report crossed my desk yesterday with your name on it. The report covered all the details of everything that went on in San Francisco concerning you and some homicide detective."

"Talbot."

"Somebody had edited the report down to the point where I didn't even know why we were interested—until I ran Quot's name through the computers and came up with the same denied-access code I'd received on all the other victims. It took me a long time to decide to even get in touch with you."

He lit another cigarette and chuckled self-deprecatingly as he waved the smoke away. "I always figured myself for some kind of outlaw in this business, Belasko. You know, James Dean with CIA clearance. That's how I worked my way up in the Agency—by being a hard-nosed son of a bitch who didn't let anything stop him." He shrugged. "I've spent two years as section chief, and during that time I've learned a lot about being a team player. When you start directing operations instead of carrying them out, it seems like your perspective changes."

"I know what you mean," Bolan replied, remembering the psychological adjustment he'd gone through with PenTeam Able when they had first been put together in Vietnam and later when he'd assembled the Death Squad in his war against the Mafia only to lose them. Other people were never as expendable as you considered yourself to be.

"A few hours ago I received notice about a team that had been almost annihilated to a man in Angola, about a heartbeat before I found out that the team had been sent there initially under orders cut with my name on them. The scuttlebutt is that these guys were also responsible for sinking a yacht in Luanda while trying to take out the owner. I don't suppose any of this is news to you."

"No."

"Shit," Bowen said in disgust. He stared over Bolan's shoulder with a blank look that told the Executioner what the CIA section chief was seeing was all internal. "I didn't want this operation," Bowen went on. "I didn't see that we had any real interest in it. Sure, the murders were of people that the Agency had employed in operations in Vietnam at one time, but what did it have to do with us now? That was before I couldn't access the files under the men's names. That was also before I got a call from an inmate of Leavenworth wanting protection. Then he turned up dead."

"He was one of the missing members of the team?"

Bowen nodded. "Yeah. My superior, Francis Crosby, has made sure that one won't hit the newspapers. The body was claimed by a convenient relative when prison records at first didn't have one listed, and is already a handful of ashes." He looked directly at Bolan. "The thing is, I think our side had the guy murdered."

"The CIA?"

"Yeah, and Crosby in particular."

"What connection does Crosby have to the murders?"

"Other than being intensely interested in every development and in keeping public information at an all-time minimum, I don't know. I referenced his file, but I think it's been purged of any mention of whatever it is we're hiding."

"So you're out in the cold?"

"To put it succinctly, yeah."

Bolan waited, knowing Bowen would have to speak what was on his mind without any prompting on his part. The guy was dealing with his own sense of moral obligations and code of conduct. And it was hard to do when you had built those ethics around an organization or around people who suddenly appeared to be something other than what you had pegged them to be.

"Crosby has put my career on the line with this thing," Bowen confided, "but I don't really give a shit about that. This job is a political son of a bitch, anyway, and there'll be another one somewhere if this one falls through," he chuckled dryly. "The problem is, Mike, I really believe in the CIA. I believe in the things we stand for. God, I got sucked into the Agency straight out of college. I didn't even know what I wanted to do with my life when I graduated. I answered an ad in the newspaper as a lark with a few of my friends. The next thing I knew a recruiter was telling me I was exactly what the Agency was looking for. If I could make the grade. Get up to speed. That's what the guy said. I never did see him again. But he made an impression on me. You know?"

"Yeah, I know. I've met Army sergeants who were lifers who did the same thing to kids. If things hadn't worked out the way they had, maybe I'd have been one of them."

Bowen grinned, but there wasn't a lot of mirth in the effort. "I don't recall much mention of military experience in your dossier, Mike, and I studied that thing hard."

"Maybe they didn't put everything in. It was a rush job."

"Yeah, right. You probably know more about this thing than I do," Bowen said as he lighted another cigarette.

"I've got a few angles I'm working on," Bolan admitted, "but until something else breaks, I'm at an impasse."

Bowen narrowed his gaze, and the warrior saw the age creep into the CIA agent's eyes, giving him a look of antiquity that was denied by the uncreased smoothness of the face.

"The hit in Angola tells me Crosby is looking for somebody," Bowen said. "The fact that all those guys got killed without even coming close to the man they were looking for tells me the somebody they're looking for is one dangerous son of a bitch. It's going to take another dangerous son of a bitch to track him down. Crosby and his goons are only going to fart around until innocent people get hurt."

"I think so, too."

Bowen shifted in the plastic booth, placing his shoulders against the back. "They've got me covered, Mike. I can't do a goddamn thing without three people checking to make sure I'm doing it right. And Crosby is keeping all the pertinent information out of my hands. It's strictly on a need-to-know basis, and I don't need to know. I've found bugs in my apartment, the second-in-command who was assigned to me would sell my ass out from under me in a heartbeat and the waitress I finally talked into sharing my bed this past week was a plant from the very start." He paused, getting control of himself. "And I'm one of the good guys."

Bolan waited, knowing there was nothing he could say.

"If I'd been on my toes, if I'd been thinking instead of trying to hotdog it, that guy in Leavenworth might still be alive. I could have gotten the warden to put him in solitary until I got there to talk to him."

"You don't know that, Greg. Orders might have been issued before you left D.C. to put this guy on ice."

"Yeah, well, by boldly going where angels fear to tread I might have put his neck in that noose earlier." Bowen blew out an angry breath. "The reason I'm telling you this is because I know you work out of Justice, but you don't work for anyone there. Brognola's a friend. I caught that the first time I worked with you guys." He sighed and looked out the window, as if undecided about what he had to say next. Then he looked back at Bolan, compassion burning in his eyes. "I guess what I need to know, Mike, is how far down in the dirt you're willing to crawl."

Maintaining unflinching eye contact, Bolan said, "I've been at the very bottom. You can't put me any farther under than I've already been before."

"I want you to know that I don't think Crosby and whoever is pulling his strings will stop short of shooting you down in the streets."

"They've already tried."

"In San Francisco?"

"Quot was the primary objective, and I was too quick for the sniper."

"Damn!" Bowen looked sick.

"You find dirt everywhere you look," Bolan said. "It's part of the system that makes the good things we do really stand out. Good and evil. You don't have one without the other no matter where you go. I try to draw lines around the innocents and fight fire with fire, hoping to maintain some kind of balance. Sometimes that's the best you can hope for, but if you don't fight for it, it won't ever come."

Bowen was silent.

Bolan sipped his coffee, unable to keep from noticing the CIA man's shaking hands.

"I can't get into those files," Bowen said. "And even if I could, Crosby would shut me down before I could do anything with what I learned." He sighed. "When I heard you were working this thing, I knew I had to talk to you. You can get things done that I can't from where I sit. I just wanted to explain things to you, let you know what I was thinking. Hell, maybe I just wanted to say it out loud to somebody so I'd know for myself." He grinned weakly. "I've never sold out the CIA before. Yet if I want to remain loyal to the spirit in which I took the job, that's exactly what I'm going to have to do."

"What have you got in mind?"

"If you've got somebody good with computers, I can set up a modem call where a good hacker can pull the files and maybe break the lock on them."

Bolan was silent for a moment, knowing the younger man was contemplating political suicide if not a more corporeal one.

"Mike?"

"Have you thought about what's going to happen if you do this?"

Bowen nodded. "Long and hard, trust me. But I like even less what will probably happen if I don't. Like I said, Mike, I took my oath seriously, and I don't intend for somebody like Crosby and whoever is jerking his chain to make me less than what I am."

"I copy," Bolan said, meeting the man's level gaze. Yeah, the big hellfire warrior could understand the CIA chief's words. They sparked a lot of kindred feelings and unlocked the paths to dozens of memories that shared that same personal conviction. "I know a guy. I figure we can set it up on a special 800 number and keep everyone off the other end of the connection."

"Fine. I'll give you a number where you can contact me when this thing's set up. Just make sure you don't drop the damn ball after I give it to you."

Bowen's grin was infectious, and Bolan felt one reflected on his lips.

"There's one other thing," Bowen said. "Provided I get the chance to live through this, I'll need a good lawyer."

"I'll do better than that," Bolan said. "I'll make sure you get a lawyer and I'll throw in a press agent." He stood and shook hands with the CIA man, his mind already outlining his next few moves. "Take care of yourself."

"You, too."

Then Bolan was out the door, wondering why it was that good people had to make sacrifices to gain any ground while evil seemed to spread without injury to itself. At the same time, he was grateful that men like Greg Bowen existed.

10

Perspiration covered Greg Bowen's palms despite the air-conditioning in the Langley data offices. He lit another cigarette as he stared through the glass walls around the computer center at the heart of the Agency's basement offices. Three shirt-sleeved operatives manned desk and computer consoles as the massive wall-size mainframes digested incoming information from all over the globe and sorted it into processing centers in less than the blink of an eye.

A distinct hum from the computers filled the air and seeped through the soles of Bowen's shoes. Naked fear coiled greasily through his stomach as he contemplated once more what he was about to do.

A glance at the bank of clocks on the wall to his left told him that it was 2:45 p.m., Virginia time. Give it another five minutes, he told himself, then commandeer a phone in the room.

The room looked sterile, like a coroner's operating room. The comparison chilled him, conjuring up disturbing images of his own mortality. He could feel his pulse beating in his temples and wondered if it would show to any of the men in the room when he entered. He ran the 800 number Belasko had given him through his mind once more, then crushed out his cigarette in the sand-filled receptacle by the door and entered.

"Hey, Greg," one of the computer operatives said as he glanced up from the greenish screen of a CRT, "what brings you down here?"

Bowen gave the man a smile and hoped it looked somewhere close to normal, or at least innocuous. This morning he had shaved a ghost of himself in the bathroom mirror. "Slumming, Freddie. It happens to us all sooner or later."

The man yawned and scooted back from his desk, rubbing his eyes with the heels of his palms. "Yeah, well, you couldn't ask to slum in finer company."

"They tell me that everywhere I go."

The computer technician grinned and patted the pockets of his white lab smock. "You got a smoke on you, Greg?"

Bowen dug out the half-empty pack he'd bought just that morning and handed it over. "Mind if I use your terminal while you smoke?"

The technician stood up and gestured to the chair. "Be my guest. Something wrong with the one in your office?"

Bowen sat in the swivel chair and placed his fingers on the keys. "No. Crosby's up there checking over the operation I'm heading, and I'm getting tired of him looking over my shoulder."

"I know what you're talking about. You should be in here when we're pulling some hot stuff in from the field."

"Like the details of what happened to the team in Angola?"

"Yeah."

"What do you know about that, Freddie?"

The man shrugged and looked uncomfortable, glancing over his shoulder at the other men in the computer center before he spoke. "Not much, Greg. A whole lot of the stuff that comes in is coded so that the tech handling it through the system doesn't know what's going on."

"I also know you guys are sometimes more in the know than you let on, Freddie."

"Yeah, well, hazard of the trade, I guess."

Bowen was silent for a moment. "You know that was supposed to be an operation passed by my office."

"Yeah."

"It wasn't, though, Freddie. Crosby set that whole thing up and used my name to cover it. I still don't know exactly what went down over there, but I do know we got four dead agents out of the deal."

The computer technician shook out a cigarette and stuck it into a corner of his mouth.

Bowen's voice was a persuasive whisper. "Come on, Freddie, don't hold out on me. Crosby has my ass hanging over the fire on this one."

"It was a hit that got busted."

"By who?"

Leaning over Bowen's shoulder, the technician acted as if he were doing some adjustments on the CRT. "By the guy they were sent after."

"One guy?"

"One guy."

"Who?"

"A man named Shane Innis."

"How does he figure into this?"

"I don't know. He's under the same lock as the dead men from the War Memorial."

"What was he doing in Angola?"

"Mercenary work. He's been running his own group over there for the past fifteen years under an alias."

"We knew that all this time?"

"No. The intel turned up on the first termination out in L.A."

"Why wasn't I told?"

"I don't know, Greg. I filed a report, but Crosby intercepted it." There was a sympathetic gleam in the technician's eyes. "Look, I'm taking a chance even telling you this much."

"I know, Freddie, and I appreciate it, but I'm up against the wall here, and I have the feeling Crosby has put me in someone else's cross hairs."

The technician was silent.

Bowen made himself be patient, knowing he couldn't push the man much further despite the casual friendship they had struck up over the years. Freddie Blankenship had been a resource for him many times while gathering background information on an operation. They'd had lunch together a few times after discovering a mutual interest in handball. Nothing set in bedrock, but it was more than you got most of the time in the Agency. He glanced at the clock and saw that it was three minutes to three. "One last question, Freddie, and I'll let you get to that cigarette."

"Okay."

"You've been here a long time, drecking through all of these files every day. Have you ever come across someone named Hacker?"

"Shit, Greg, do you think Hacker's involved in this?"

"I'm not sure. I have reason to believe he was fifteen years ago."

"During the war?"

Bowen nodded, noticing how the pasty whiteness of the technician's face had faded even more.

"Hacker did a lot of behind-the-scene stuff over there. It's possible. Most of his operations have been lost or locked over the years."

"Who is he, Freddie?"

"A fucking ghost," the technician assured him. "Hacker's a code name. I don't even know if he's still with the Agency, but if he is, keep the hell away from him. I've heard rumors over the years that Hacker was in on the plot to put J. Edgar Hoover away when the FBI refused to keep sharing all the information their illegal wiretaps and surveillances turned up on guys like the Kennedys, King and other people working out of Capitol Hill." He paused. "I mean it, Greg, if you find out Hacker's involved, you better dig a hole and pull it in after you."

Bowen watched the man walk away, trying to sort through the information. Hacker. The name had turned up, but he didn't know if the man behind the name was still alive. But the name still commanded power and fear. On both sides of the line.

Lifting the phone, he punched in the 800 number, then turned his attention to the CRT. His fingers drifted across the computer keys, calling up the locked files containing the information on the War Memorial murders.

"Hello?"

The voice at the other end of the connection sounded tinny and far away, neutered and devoid of any real life. The whir, hiss and buzz of white noise filled the line.

"Ready?" Bowen breathed into the phone.

"Yes."

His fingers moved almost by themselves, chaining the files together, then adding Hacker's name to the list. Dumping the access into memory mode, he punched up the menu and ordered a modem connect, knowing somewhere in the building alarms were going off, signaling an unauthorized outgoing computer link. He placed the receiver onto the model with a shaking hand, knowing he had done everything he could do and hoping it would be enough to get Belasko something to work with.

"Hey!" one of the terminal operators shouted.

Glancing at the CRT in front of him, Bowen saw the screen had started flashing, signaling an unauthorized use. Then the black words printed across the emerald screen abruptly broke into a variegated network of blocks, squares and dots, alternately changing from gray to white to black as they continued an unintelligible march from top to bottom.

"Goddamn it!" the terminal operator yelled as he stood up and glanced around the room. "Somebody's broken into the computers." He turned startled eyes on the other operator. "Find out where it's coming from. Now!"

Bowen moved, dragging the stainless-steel Taurus .357 Magnum from his shoulder holster. He thumbed the hammer back, getting the attention of the two other men immediately. "Sit down," he ordered.

"What the hell do you think you're doing?" the technician bellowed as he started forward.

Placing a foot on the front of the man's desk, Bowen kicked out hard. The desk slid across the tiled floor, uncarpeted because of the risk of static electricity interfering with the computer's operations, and slammed into the man, knocking him across his chair. Bowen lifted the .357 to full arm's extension.

"You're crazy," the other technician said.

"Shut up!" Bowen ordered. He flicked a quick glance at the CRT, watching the shapes continue their march down the screen. Belasko's man was getting the information, but was it going to be in any form he could use? He felt perspiration trickle down the back of his neck. He couldn't be doing this for nothing, could he? How long would it take to drain all the files off?

Movement darkened the doorway, and he tracked the revolver automatically.

Freddie.

"Greg, what the hell are you doing?"

"I'm not going to hurt anybody if you'll just do as I say," Bowen said calmly. "Just get over against that wall with the others."

Before Freddie could move, another man slid behind him and elbowed the technician out of the way. Bowen locked eyes with Francis Crosby as he put the front sight over the older man's heart.

Crosby's dark eyes flashed with rage. He didn't look like a killer. Dressed in an immaculately cut dark suit and with his gray-white hair neatly in place, Crosby looked more like a church deacon than a CIA agent. Without saying a word, Crosby reached under his jacket and took a .38 S&W Chiefs Special from his right hip. His eyes never dropped to consider the already-drawn .357.

Crosby knew he wouldn't drop the hammer, Bowen realized, at the same frozen moment realizing the older agent had no such compunction at all himself.

Bowen heard the dry snaps of the .38, then felt the impacts shake through his abdomen, driving him backward. He lost the Taurus somewhere on the way down as sensation began to fade away from him. He sprawled on his back, unable to move, wondering if one of the bullets that had hit him had injured his spine and paralyzed him. He glanced at the CRT, watching the gray-white-black blocks filtering down the screen. Abruptly the monitor fragmented. Bowen was only dimly aware of the explosion of Crosby's third shot as it destroyed the CRT. Pieces flipped and flashed through the air, raining down all around him.

He wondered if Belasko had had enough time to pull the necessary information free of the computer. Then the room seemed to spin around him and swallow him whole.

INNIS STOOD in the shadows near the pier, taking in the smells of the sea and the drifting sounds that fell around him through the senses the years of being in the jungles had wired into his central nervous system.

He'd dressed casually for the meeting, wearing jeans, sandals and a loose-fitting Hawaiian shirt that covered the Colt Officer's .45 automatic tucked into a belly holster. He'd also acquired a TEC-22 Scorpion converted to full-auto and a Gerber MkI boot knife. The knife was sheathed near his ankle under the jeans; the machine pistol was secured in the Adidas gym bag he carried, along with extra ammunition.

For almost twenty minutes he had drifted along the various slips, keeping watch over the smooth blue sea as gaily colored craft made their way by diesel engine or by canvas, searching for the familiar lines of Judson's yacht among them. Sailing was a common bond Innis hadn't known they'd shared until after the war, but he hadn't hesitated about using the knowledge to bind Judson to him even more tightly. Some of the first money he'd made from the South African work had been "loaned" to Judson to purchase the yacht. Upkeep on the vessel was expensive, as well, and Judson would have been hard-pressed to manage it himself.

Innis hadn't minded the "loans" that were never paid back. Judson's continued connections with certain CIA people and State Department people were worth that, as well as Judson's ability to coordinate messages between the other members of the Hawks.

Money had never been an issue with Innis. As long as there was plenty of it to attend to his needs, he was happy. But the war, the killing, the feel of someone's pulse under his thumb as he took that person's life away, that was what he thrived on. You couldn't replace that feeling of ultimate power, nor could you buy it. You had to reach out for it yourself and take it—kicking and screaming—any way you could.

Innis knew Judson had never understood that about him, and had convinced himself that the trait was something the CIA operations or Vietnam had brought out in him.

It was in Vietnam that he became aware of the intense blood lust that dwelled inside him, and that he once again got the chance to form his own team—the Hawks, who'd earned the nickname Satan's Backup. He still didn't know exactly where the name had come from. Perhaps it was something Hacker had dreamed up, or maybe it was derived from the whispers the CIA controls over the operations made concerning the violence Innis demanded of his men. At any rate, Innis had made sure they continued to earn the name.

Now the CIA was talking about Satan's Backup again. At least some of them were—the ones Hacker had let into the inner circle of the operation to shut the team down.

Innis grinned to himself.

Hacker.

How much of a threat was the CIA man? Hacker had been old during the war. Had the years dulled the man's wits? Maybe.

Innis dismissed the CIA man for the moment. The real danger lay in the identity of the man who had killed Lawrence and the others. Innis knew Hacker. He'd worked for the man, had learned his thoughts enough to outplan and outthink him. The most dangerous enemy a man could have was one he did *not* know. Like the hunter who had locked into a killzone with the Hawks for reasons of his own.

But Judson had sounded convinced he had an idea of who the man might be. Even at that, the knowledge might not be needed. Innis knew he and his group would be leaving Miami within hours after the last man arrived. Perhaps the unknown man would remain that: unknown and ultimately ineffectual just as Hacker's efforts were doomed to be.

Control. So much of Innis's life had depended on it. Control of himself and of those around him. Yet, as necessary as it was, it also seemed to come naturally. The hunter had broken their cover, carefully placed all these years despite the CIA's best effort to find them, and—for a moment—he had broken the control Innis had over his own life.

But it wouldn't remain that way for long. New life was waiting for them all in Cambodia, had been waiting for fifteen years thanks to some of his planning at the end of the war. True, not everything had worked out the way he had wanted it to, but now it seemed like everything had been for the best all the same. He grinned. In fact, he couldn't have planned it any better.

And he couldn't have put a better edge on the Hawks if he'd tried. Most of them had fought with him on and off in the South African campaigns; but most of them had been motivated by financial reasons or because they missed the taste of the action. Now, with the hunter and the CIA on their asses, they were as motivated as hell.

Once they touched down in Cambodia, Innis figured most of the CIA movement would break off. It was enough that an annual budget of five million dollars had been established in the United States for use by the rebels in Cambodia struggling against Communist rule without tossing American agents in, as well.

But would that stop the hunter?

Innis didn't think so. This smacked of something even more personal than the grudge Hacker and the CIA held against Satan's Backup. But who would have waited fifteen years to start seeking them out? Or had there been other factors involved? The VC who had had the chance to meet them in Vietnam had died. And why would they begin the hunt now? Where would they have found the new identities of the Hawks?

He shifted the gym bag to his other hand as the familiar lines of Judson's yacht powered into position two slips down. Innis felt his jungle senses come alive as he watched two young boys jump lithely to the pier and secure the yacht's lines. No one appeared to be interested in the craft.

Nudging the zipper of the gym bag open so that he could easily reach the machine pistol, Innis strode down the length of the slip as the boys fitted a boarding ramp to the side of the yacht. The CIA wasn't looking for him here. Once they had penetrated the Manchester cover in Angola, he knew they would have plenty of history to deal with dragging the complete story of his South African operations from the various sources in that country. Hacker and his men would be moving more slowly now, less aggressively. The dead men he had left them in Luanda would have taught them that. They would search for him in Africa, never knowing until it was too late that he had taken passage back to Miami. There were no records anywhere that Manchester had ever left the continent.

The boys removed the boarding ramp as soon as he crossed it. Innis paused for a moment, staring across the numerous houseboats, fishing boats and yachts bobbing gently in their private slips, trying to trace the niggling feeling at the base of his skull.

Watched.

He could feel it, and he was sure it wasn't Hacker or any of Hacker's men. Innis had been accustomed to having CIA people breathing down his neck. This wasn't the same response.

The feeling that resonated within him now stuck a more primeval chord that found harmonious resolution with the unnamed sense. He felt the gentle swell of the deck beneath his feet, felt his body unconsciously responding to compensate for the movement. Then the feeling vanished as quickly as the snapping of a wire.

In its place the feeling of absence was almost as noticeable, like an empty tooth socket. Nature abhorred a vacuum. Innis could remember reading that somewhere, and realized this hunt was something that existed at a level akin to nature. It wasn't Hacker's kind of work; not murder adorned with pseudo-political motivations to make it more palatable. But who was truly the hunter and the hunted remained to be seen.

Innis was aware of his heartbeat's rapidity and smiled to himself, hoping when he finally met his pursuer that it would be a match worthy of him. He didn't want his adversary to die too quickly.

"Shane?"

Innis turned to face Judson, finding the older man seated in the wheelchair he'd been confined to for the past handful of years. The man looked unhealthy, like a lump of dough filled with bones as thin as wire hangers, and dusted on top with cottony gray hair. Taking the skeletal hand Judson offered, Innis thought it felt more like a claw than a hand against his own muscular palm, the physical differences between the two of them even more pronounced. Less than ten years separated them, yet Innis knew his physical state would never sink as low as Judson's had. It wasn't just a difference in genes, he had decided a long time ago. It was the way they chose to live life. Judson was timid and shied away from conflict, physical as well as mental; Innis gloried in both.

"Tell me about the boy," Innis said.

"There's not much I know, Shane," Judson said as he rested his elbows on the arms of the wheelchair. "He called himself Khoi. He was one of the boys Dodson hired on for the summer to swamp boats and do repair work at the boating service I use. He's Vietnamese. Short and wiry, with close-cropped black hair. Since he started to work for me as a groundskeeper, he grew one of those pigtail things the teenagers seem to be partial to these days. I don't think he was exceptionally receptive to it, but it helped him blend in with everyone around him."

"And that was important?"

Judson tapped nervous fingertips against the chair. "Now that I look back on it, yes, it does strike me that way. He remained quiet the whole time I knew him. I didn't figure he'd been in the States long, by the way he acted, but he spoke good English."

"Like maybe he'd learned it somewhere else?"

"Meaning Vietnam?"

Innis nodded.

"But who would send one lone boy over here in the hopes of finding American GIs who had been reported killed in action somewhere over Cambodia?"

"That I don't know." Innis frowned as he looked out over the other craft crowded around them. He no longer felt the watchful eyes on him, but he knew the hunter wasn't far away. Why would one boy attempt to find

Satan's Backup let alone even know of it? "How old would you say this kid was, Drew?"

"Twenty, twenty-five, maybe older. I never did get good at guessing their ages."

"How did he find out where Lawrence and the others were?"

The left side of Judson's face twitched and he looked away from Innis. "He found part of the files I've maintained on the team."

"How?"

"I don't now. In fact, I didn't know he'd found the files until after Lawrence was killed. Then I left word for you in drops we use for emergencies, but you never got back to me. I assume you never got the messages."

Innis shook his head.

"The only way I knew was because he'd copied the addresses from the files, and the impression of the pencil he'd used imprinted against the manila folders."

"But he knew where to look to being with," Innis said. "That should tell us something."

Judson seemed relieved that Innis wasn't going to focus on the security of the files.

"How many of the team were compromised in those files?" Innis asked.

"Five."

"And three of them have been terminated?"

"Yes."

Innis shifted perspectives, taking in the view on the other side of Judson's yacht. The turbines whined and the deck of the craft shimmied as the power was reversed, forcing it back toward the openness of the sea. "What about the other two men?"

"No attempts were made on their lives. They've secured safe quarters until the team gets together tonight."

"Do they know security on your files was compromised?"

"No. I've told them nothing other than your orders to meet at the warehouse tonight."

"And the other half of the files weren't touched?"

"No."

Innis considered that.

"Maybe he thought I suspected something," Judson said.

"Did you?"

"No." Judson's reply was weak, and anxiety in his voice more apparent.

Then why would this guy think that? Innis asked himself, knowing the older man was only trying to save face and not really giving a damn. Judson had always been interested in the appearance of things more than how things were done. Innis knew the man had often softened the brutality of the reports he had turned in, editing out anything that might have compromised the integrity of the team, finally resorting to making hard copy from a tape-recorded statement Innis had given him.

Judson's wheelchair rolled slightly, making the man grab the wheels suddenly with a curse, then struggle to set the brake.

The crux of the problem was that the hunter knew about the Hawks to begin with, and knew as well that the team was still alive. Innis had to guess at how much more the man, or boy, knew. Maybe the hunter even knew about Cambodia. It was something to take into consideration while figuring the logistics of the team's last operation. And, like all the others, this one was going to be a do-or-die mission.

"Maybe nothing else will happen," Judson said hopefully. "From some of the intel I've been able to gather, Drake wounded the man who killed him."

Innis shook his head. "He's still alive, and he's still out there. He's just waiting for the right opening to make his move." He smiled in anticipation, wondering which was the more thrilling: hunting or being hunted? Both put an edge on life, and both required the ultimate focus of the participant's being. His blood beat in primeval cadence, warming him despite the cooling flush coming off the sea.

The hunter was waiting, biding his time.

Innis smiled again because the hunter couldn't know the prey was waiting, as well, even anticipating the moment of the kill.

MACK BOLAN PEELED an orange methodically as he watched Kurtzman struggling to outthink the CIA file's lock. Shapes and colors darted across the monitor in front of the big man, darting and shimmering as thoughts and logic pried and pushed at the program's battlements with invisible fingers.

Dropping the last of the orange peel into the trash can, Bolan broke the fruit in half and freed a wedge. The cool, crisp, citrus taste exploded inside his mouth, bringing with it the first sensory impression that was something other than visual for almost an hour. He savored it as he continued to watch the screen over one of the Bear's broad shoulders.

"Mack." Kurtzman's voice sounded hushed. His fingers were resting on the bottom of the computer keyboard.

Bolan moved forward, gazing at the monitor. Lines of text were scrolling upward. "You're in."

"Yeah." Kurtzman grinned like a kid with an ice-cream cone. "God, I was about ready to give up when pieces of this thing started to fall together in my head."

"What have you got?"

Kurtzman shrugged. "Names, dates, places, pictures. It looks like the whole damn mess." He paused. "It'll take me a few minutes to get it together for you. When I broke into the program, I fractured a few of the menus and I'll have to recreate them or absorb them into another function."

Bolan nodded, checking the time on his watch and finding that it was a few minutes past five. Brognola should have some intel on Bowen by now. "I'll be back in a few minutes."

Kurtzman grunted an unintelligible reply.

The warrior used the phone in the hallway outside Kurtzman's lab. After identifying himself, he asked about Bowen.

"It's not good, Striker. According to the reports I've been able to overhear, an agent named Francis Crosby found out the computer security had been breached and went to check on it himself. When he arrived in the computer room, Bowen had his gun out and was menacing the technicians on duty. Crosby felt he had no choice, that Bowen had flipped out, and shot him."

"How bad is it, Hal?"

"Two rounds in the abdominal region," Brognola said. "They still have him on a table at Walter Reed, but I don't think they expect him to make it."

"What do you know about Crosby?" Bolan focused on his train of thought, blocking out the images of Bowen from this morning. He had learned a long time ago that warriors didn't often have the time to grieve or reflect on the passing of a comrade in arms immediately and had to settle for making time in the future.

"Not much, Striker. Crosby's one of the boys Langley keeps a lid on. He's been involved in a number of hot spots all across the globe."

"Can we tie the Hacker name to him?"

"Maybe, but it's not Crosby's name. From the poop I received from an acquaintance in the Agency this afternoon while getting the details about Bowen's arrest, Crosby isn't far removed from Hacker. Hacker himself is some kind of myth at the Agency—you can't lay a finger on the guy. The word I get is that Hacker's a holdover from the JFK regime, involved in the Bay of Pigs and the whole cold war front. Strictly an old school spy."

"Has the story about Bowen hit the media yet?"

"No. Langley's keeping all information in-house until they figure what kind of angle they're going to try to sell it as."

"And part of that depends on whether Bowen lives through the surgery."

"Yeah."

Bolan was silent for a moment, reflecting on all the secrets the CIA was already trying to keep from public view.

"It's a crappy way to do business," Brognola said. "The official gossip I heard was that if Bowen doesn't survive, the Agency's going to sell him and his career down the river and paint him out as a mole, then gussy Crosby up as the guy who saved the CIA. The unofficial gossip is that Crosby was judged as overreacting and is going to be assigned a rubber room until his superiors figure out what to do with him."

"And in the meantime they're not interested in finding out why Crosby overreacted?"

"No. The CIA's interested in salvaging anything from this, Striker. They're at the amputation stage—cut off anything that looks tainted and try to save the whole."

"So they can afford to lose Bowen even though the man was working to get the information that had been hidden since the beginning of this operation."

"It's not a pretty business we're involved in here," Brognola replied gruffly.

Bolan considered the situation for a moment, twisting all the variables through the strategies open to him. If he was one of Bowen's superiors, would he be willing to kick back and let the man survive the operation if he was able? No. Not without knowing how much Bowen knew about the operation being run under the cover the Agency was laying down. Which meant the CIA section chief's life was in danger again the minute he was taken to post-op. "What can Justice do to provide Bowen with protection while he's in the hospital?"

"Officially?"

"It's the only way we can keep his room restricted from anyone else Hacker might send after him."

"You think it would come to that?"

"Put yourself in Hacker's shoes for a moment, Hal."

Brognola paused. "Okay. What have you got in mind?"

"Force the CIA into giving Bowen up as a security risk, then get someone from Enforcement to arrest Bowen the minute he goes up to post-op."

"For what?"

"Conspiracy to undermine an investigation by the Justice Department into matters concerning national security. Remember, one of Justice's guys belonged to the group the CIA is trying to keep covered up. The Agency isn't supposed to operate domestically according to their 1947 charter, so jurisdiction in this investigation would belong to Justice. Not the CIA. The Agency would have to prove a stronger case against Bowen than they have so far to even get their foot in the door."

"And to do that they'd have to release details of the files Bowen was attempting to swipe, which they aren't going to be willing to do."

"That's the way I figure it." Bolan prodded his logic, trying to punch holes in the plan of action he'd suggested. It would at least confuse the issue long enough to allow him to take the pressure off the current situation and start Hacker and his followers scrambling in a new direction.

"I'll get Gunnar Greggson on it as soon as we clear the line," Brognola promised. "I didn't think about that option. I've been busy trying to figure out a way to salvage the man and his career. He put a lot on the line for us when he offered to break into those files."

"He knew that going in, Hal. But no matter what the final upshot of the political or career situation is, I want to save the man if we're able."

"Agreed."

"I'm bringing in a reporter, too," Bolan said.

"Anyone I know?"

"Susan Landry. She's going to have the gist of the investigation, sans details, from an as yet 'undisclosed' source. Maybe together, with your team working security, Susan building a case for Bowen in the media, and my applying pressure where I can behind the scenes, we can save the man."

"Okay, I'll arrange clearance for her to visit his room."

"Take care of him, Hal." Bolan broke the connection and went back to see what Kurtzman had been able to uncover from the stolen CIA data.

11

"Meet former Army Major Shane J. Innis," Kurtzman said as he waved to the screen at the other end of the room.

Bolan looked at the man's profile presented in black and white. "Alias Timothy Manchester."

"Yeah. You saw the picture the ID program generated when I took twenty years off this guy's age?"

Bolan nodded.

"You couldn't ask for a better comparison," Kurtzman said as he tapped buttons on his keyboard. Details of personal and military life scrolled across the screen in quick response, followed by those of the men who had served under Innis, who had died in battle or found another way out.

Bolan followed the script easily, noting the man's sudden field promotion to major after being assigned to Project Counterpunch under a CIA agent code-named Hacker in 1962.

According to the files, Innis hadn't been an ideal soldier while stationed in Vietnam or even during boot camp. He was short-tempered, disrespectful and violent. A loner. But field observations by different lieutenants revealed another side of Innis. The man was deadly in the war zones, a natural killer with a zest for his work. Some of those reports had included recommendations that Innis be transferred back to the States and hospitalized for his tendencies toward unrestricted violence.

Apparently a man with those tendencies was exactly who Hacker had been looking for.

"It's all here," Kurtzman said in a subdued voice. "I looked it over while you were on the phone with Hal. The CIA, under Hacker, put a twelve-man team—code-named Hawks—into operation against the Vietcong before American involvement was authorized by President Johnson. Here's a list of strikes the team made against the North Vietnamese." He tapped the keyboard.

Places and dates scrolled across the screen, with the objectives outlined briefly below as well as the success or failure of the mission. There were no critical failures. Most of the operations were regarding termination of high-ranking North Vietnamese military people, as well as rescue maneuvers of CIA personnel and attacks on ammo dumps.

From the list, Bolan gathered the team hadn't done anything he and other Special Forces groups hadn't been asked to do later in the war, except that they did it without the official sanction of the American and South Vietnamese governments.

Bolan shook his head as he tried to figure out why the CIA would go to such lengths to hide the files. "This isn't anything the American people haven't expected before, Aaron. Why the secrecy?"

"Because of this." Kurtzman produced another list, scrolling through it more slowly. "Take a look at the names. Maybe you're not familiar with many of them, but you'll recognize enough of them to get the main thrust of these terminations."

Bolan scanned the list, noticing female Vietnamese names often with the entries of their husbands and fathers and, less often, with their sons and daughters. "These are South Vietnamese officials."

Kurtzman nodded. "Hacker wanted the team to be independent of every other military operation going on in Vietnam, and he got it that way. I tried to find out if someone in Washington authorized the hits, but if someone did, they kept the names and the facts concealed."

"So Hacker's group was hitting South Vietnamese targets, as well."

"Yeah."

Bolan stared at the list, feeling the rage boil up inside him. He had believed in the war just as Bowen had believed in the good things the CIA stood for. He had fought hard, had shed his blood, had seen good men die in those jungles. "Hacker used Innis and his men to escalate American involvement in the war effort," he said.

"That's the way I read it, too," Kurtzman said. "I can remember reading some of the newspaper articles concerning the people on this list. Take that Vietnamese ambassador there. His wife was killed before him. She was discovered in their motel room in Saigon with her throat cut after being gang-raped while her husband attended a joint South Vietnamese-American meeting in 1963." He caused the script to scroll backward until the wife's name was revealed. "It caused a big stir when it reached American newspapers, as an example of the godless communism that was being spread by the North Vietnamese. Notice the dates involved on this list. See how the number of hits tapers off dramatically once American troops were fielded."

"Yeah. I see."

"This is what they were hiding," Kurtzman said. "I don't know how many people in the CIA actually know about this file, but evidently word has gone down that this was to be left undisturbed."

"Makes you wonder why it was never destroyed, doesn't it?"

"It does until you take into consideration that, whoever he really is, Hacker was probably using this as part of his survival portfolio. A guy as gutsy as this has probably stepped on a lot of political toes on his way to the top. It took a lot for me to crack this thing, Striker. If I didn't have the background I do, if I didn't have the sheer computer power backing me that I do, I don't think I could have gotten inside this thing." Kurtzman shrugged. "Hacker probably thought he had everything under wraps."

"Until members of Innis's team started turning up dead."

"And until Bowen managed to get the information to us." Kurtzman looked at Bolan. "How is Bowen?"

"Not too good. The doctors don't expect him to pull through."

"Jeez, that's too bad."

"Yeah." Bolan shifted, putting the depressing thoughts out of his mind as he came to grips with the strategies left open to him by the information the CIA section chief had managed to uncover. Hacker couldn't let it end here; neither could Innis or his men. "What happened in 1975?"

Kurtzman tapped the keyboard. "Innis and his team were reported shot down somewhere over Cambodia. Hacker sent in a CIA patrol to search for the wreckage days later when an informer brought them word of where the plane went down. According to the eyes-only report, all of Innis's team was accounted for."

"How?"

"Dog tags. The bodies had been burned beyond recognition."

"Convenient."

"Yeah, as hell."

"I wonder how Hacker felt when the first man in L.A. was found."

Kurtzman's smile was without mirth. "Probably about the way you would expect him to feel. Like a ghost had climbed out of the grave."

"Hacker bought the death scene just like that? He should know from experience how easy it would have been to leave the dog tags on corpses brought along for that specific purpose and set fire to the wreckage later."

"He didn't buy it at first. There are reports in this file from other agents who went in later to recheck the story. By that time Cambodia had been taken over by the Khmer Rouge. You know the score on that place, Striker—a million, maybe two million people may have been killed during Pol Pot's reign. When we pulled out of Vietnam, those people went under, too. It wasn't until the Vietnamese invaded in December 1978 that the country even began to recover a semblance of sanity."

"How did Innis and his men get a plane of their own?"

"They stole it from Tan Son Nhut Airport, from a CIA operative helping remove some of the Agency's highly placed allies in the South Vietnamese government. And that isn't all." Kurtzman locked eyes with Bolan. "The same day they took the plane, during the confusion of the pending evacuation, Innis and his men hit a South Vietnamese bank and successfully heisted a cool five million in gold and American currency."

"Hacker had cut orders to get out of the operation with a clean slate."

Kurtzman nodded. "As clean as possible, under the circumstances."

"Operation Mad Dog," Bolan said, remembering Quot's words before the CIA sniper had killed the crack dealer.

"Right."

"How did Innis find out about Mad Dog?"

"From his military control."

"Hacker had to work the operations through a military liaison?"

"Yes. A man named Drew Judson." Kurtzman tapped the keyboard and a new picture formed on the screen. Judson looked to be in his late thirties in the black-and-white still, with light-colored hair and a boyish grin.

"Now for the after picture," Kurtzman said. "I tracked into his file, which is still accessible through normal channels, though purged of any mention of the Hawks." The new picture was in color, revealing a man ravaged by time. In this photo Judson was seated in a wheelchair at some kind of banquet.

"What's his story?" Bolan asked.

"Early retirement after the war," Kurtzman said, "and I'm sure we can assume Hacker had a hand in that. Why he left Judson alive is a puzzle to me."

"Unless Hacker left Judson alive as bait for Innis."

"Possibly. At any rate, Judson has led a quiet life in Miami. At least it's been a quiet life on the surface. I turned up a number of inquiries the Internal Revenue Service has had concerning the money Judson has been spending since his retirement. Apparently there are some discrepancies in the stock portfolio he's built since the war. The dividends he's been reporting add up to more than the investments have actually been paying off. Currently he's still being audited for 1984 through the present year. The case will probably settle sometime after his death. The man's in poor health."

"Why would Judson warn Innis?"

"There's nothing in the files to indicate a reason. Evidently Hacker didn't understand it, either."

"Did the CIA file contain anything about the wealth Judson seemed able to get his hands on?"

"No. I'm assuming they didn't know about it. Perhaps they didn't access Judson's personal files from the IRS the way I did. I usually put together a pretty comprehensive package for you when I do a background check on someone."

"It's always appreciated, Aaron, believe me."

The big man shrugged it away.

"Loyalty," Bolan mused out loud. "That could have been the motivation behind Judson's interference in Mad Dog."

"It could have."

"And it's certainly the tie that has bound Innis's men to him. They were a breed apart. Hacker had to have ground that into their mentality from the beginning of the project. He couldn't count on someone like Innis twisting that very conditioning around to his own uses. Or maybe it didn't matter. Maybe Hacker had planned from the beginning that the team was to have been expendable. But the loyalty, the bonds that were forged by the nature of the operations they undertook, are a reflection of what Hacker forced those men to become."

"Hey, Striker, these guys are no angels, believe me. I've got their bios on file here, as well as some accounts by various CIA controls on different operations who didn't hesitate to point out the cruelty in the Hawks—mutilations, rapes, torture, unnecessary killing. It's all in there."

"That's not what I'm talking about, Aaron. I'm talking about the power of loyalty, about the way Hacker left that team cut off from any outside influences or reprimands. Loyalty given through trust by itself is without the taint of good or evil. Only the person commanding that loyalty is what determines the good or evil of the actions that follow. Bowen was being loyal to his vision of what the CIA stands for when he helped us get these files, even to the point of dying if that's what it took. We all find loyalties within ourselves, and we draw lines around those loyalties, letting experience and moral beliefs temper the limits to which we give it. Hacker's abandoning of those men strengthened Innis's control over them. Most of the guys involved in the Hawks were young men, inexperienced in the ways of war, and whatever moral convictions they carried with them into battle evidently sloughed away easily."

"Which leaves you where?" Kurtzman asked.

"Wondering," Bolan replied. "Someone's stalking those men. They know it and I know it. But whoever their hunter is knows those men will ultimately band together under Innis. In my judgment Innis isn't bound by any loyalty toward his men. Sure, he's used them off and on in his mercenary work. The autopsies of the dead men we've recovered bear that out. So what makes the stalker so sure Innis will involve himself with them again, especially knowing someone has tumbled to the fact the group still exists? Obviously Innis needs them to further his own goals."

"You're painting a picture of one callous son of a bitch," Kurtzman said.

Bolan shook his head. "The picture's already in place, Aaron. I'm just reading the writing on the wall." He paused. "How much money did you say the team took from Saigon?"

"Five million in American currency and gold."

"How much of it was in gold?"

Kurtzman sifted through the information for a moment. "Over half of it. I can't be any more precise than that with the files I've got."

"Figuring by today's prices, you're still talking about over four or five hundred pounds of gold," Bolan said. "Considering that the team had been shot down over hostile territory and probably had no plans laid for getting out of that country, knowing Hacker and his men would be dogging their heels, what would you say their chances of getting out of Cambodia with the gold would be?"

"Practically nil."

Bolan nodded. "What about the financial histories of the dead men? Is there anything in there to indicate any kind of wealth like that?"

"If there had been, Striker, it would have been in those files I prepped for you."

Bolan turned it over in his mind again. Innis and his team had to have left the gold behind, despite the planning and the twelve extra bodies they had brought with them. They couldn't have known they would be shot down. The theory scanned, providing motivation for Innis to regroup the team, which seemed to be the objective of the man stalking them. It also meant the hunter knew about the gold that had been left in Cambodia. But how? He still had no angle for that at all.

And what was Judson's part in all of this, including the unexplained wealth the man had shown? None of the members of the team would have funded the man. So far none of them had shown the resources needed for that, which left Innis and his mercenary work in South Africa.

He obviously had the resources, but why Judson? For the contacts the man retained in Military Intelligence? Yeah, but could the connection be carried farther than that? Maybe. Perhaps even as far as a go-between for Innis and the remaining members of the team. Judson would be an additional buffer between Innis and whoever might choose to pursue him. And Judson was a public figure, not in hiding the way the other men were. Innis could have other people watching Judson to make sure no one got too close to the man.

Glancing back at Kurtzman, Bolan asked, "Can you get me Drew Judson's current address in Miami?"

The big man nodded and turned to the task.

Bolan stared at the screen covered with secrets the CIA had kept buried for the past fifteen years, wondering if that information was going to cost a good man his life. He couldn't help but think about Major Shane Innis, realizing what the man did in Vietnam was based on the same skills he had learned in the jungles himself. If he did manage to close in on the Hawks, the warrior hoped he'd be skilled enough to take them out when the time came. The jungle. It had begun there for all of them. Even the hunter. Bolan was sure of that.

Now it was beginning to look as if it would find an ending there, too. One way or another.

KHOI LEFT THE CAMARO parked a half-dozen blocks from his target site. He drew his trench coat tightly around him and charted a path through the buildings that kept him in the night's shadows.

The M-16 under his coat was mounted with an M-203 grenade launcher. Clips for the rifle and three high-explosive rounds for the M-203 were in pouches belted at his waist. The Glock was buried deep in one of the trench coat's pockets, purely as a backup measure.

He wiped perspiration from his forehead, feeling the slow burn of a slight fever throb into his temples. The wound in his thigh still ached, but the pain was muted by the codeine tablets he was taking along with the penicillin.

He limped slightly as he moved, but tonight he didn't intend to get close enough to have to react with any kind of speed. By choosing the warehouse to have their meeting, Innis had put himself and his men in a place where a force of one could attack the many.

Khoi paused in his advance, resting most of his weight on the uninjured leg as he surveyed his target. The warehouse was owned by Drew Judson, though Khoi didn't think many people were aware of that fact. He had chanced across the name in the bundle of papers he had uncovered while searching for the names of the men in the Hawks.

In the beginning he had assumed Innis would meet with his men at Judson's home, and he had been afraid because he had seen the CIA men guarding the house. One of them was a man he had noticed before, while he was still employed doing the landscaping around the house. One of the smugglers Khoi knew had identified the man while the agency was watching Judson's yacht.

The CIA was looking for Innis as diligently as he was. Khoi had expected that response when he started the chain of events that had led to this place. It had been a calculated risk, but one he had been willing to take.

The warehouse facing the sea was an old hulk when compared to the sheet metal buildings that flanked it. The signs above the entrance door in the front and the exit in the rear had once read Harrison's Marine Salvage, but the salt air and passage of time had washed the red tint from the paint, leaving only a brick-colored stain behind.

The warehouse remained dark, even though Khoi knew the men had gathered inside—except for Judson, who had stayed at his home to keep the CIA guards company and give them something to report.

Khoi had seen Innis earlier, when he had boarded Judson's yacht. Hunter and hunted. They both played a part no matter how fate ultimately cast their roles.

Taking the M-16 from under the trench coat, Khoi fed the first high-explosive round into the grenade launcher and placed the remaining two on top of the crate he'd chosen for cover. He sighted, then squeezed the trigger of the M-203 carefully, riding out the recoil as he reached for his next round.

Sound thundered through the night, wiping away the vagrant noises of houseboat parties floating across the sea. The warehouse came apart as automatic weapons chattered to life.

Round number two flitted neatly through the hole opened up in the back wall by round number one. Smoke carried out of the gaping wreckage, becoming a backdrop to the yellow flares of muzzle-flashes.

Khoi fired the third round into the center of the peaked roof, feeling satisfaction when the structure swayed unsteadily, then collapsed. He hoped Innis was still alive, otherwise the remainder of the team might choose to flee rather than attempt the return to Cambodia.

Gritting his teeth against the pain in his leg, Khoi pushed himself into a standing position and tucked the M-16 back under the trench coat.

He watched the spreading fire for a moment, seeing a few scurrying figures bolt from the target site. Then, for only an instant, the orange and yellow flames limned Innis's features.

Satisfied that his quarry still lived, Khoi turned and limped back to the Camaro, grateful he would be able to rest during the flight he had arranged back to Cambodia. He would need all of his resources to fight Innis and his men in the deathgrounds he had chosen.

BOLAN STOOD in the background, leaning against the bumper of the Jeep Brognola had provided for him on this end of the jump to Miami. Fire fighters were keeping spectators back as they sifted through the wreckage of the burning warehouse. Shimmering reflections of the dying blaze still danced across the surface of the ocean to Bolan's left.

After flashing his Justice ID, he'd found out from one of the Miami policemen that the charges that had devastated the warehouse had been set off almost twenty minutes ago, and so far no one had any idea what had happened.

Using the mobile phone in the Cherokee, Bolan had quickly found out that the warehouse had belonged to Drew Judson, though the information was almost lost under a maze of paperwork. Kurtzman had been tenacious about the search, and Bolan had been sure of his gut feeling.

Maybe the fire fighters and the police weren't sure of what had gone wrong in the building, but the Executioner had seen plenty of the destructive forces unleashed by a man with a grenade launcher.

A short, broad man separated himself from the group of plainclothes policemen standing beside one of the fire engines and walked toward Bolan. The combined whirling lights of the official vehicles painted ruby and sapphire stripes across the faces of the curious onlookers.

The plainclothes officer came to a stop in front of Bolan and took another drag on his cigar as he gazed speculatively at the Executioner. The tip of the cigar flared into an angry orange coal for a moment, then faded away.

"One of the uniforms told me you were from the Justice Department," the man said.

Bolan nodded and produced his ID. "The name's Mike Belasko."

The cop took another puff and nodded. "He also told me you were looking for somebody who might have been in that warehouse when it went up."

"He told you right."

"My name's Sergeant Vic Dansby. I work homicide out of the South."

"Homicide doesn't usually work arson cases."

Dansby shook his head. "We're not working one now." He pointed toward the warehouse with his cigar. "The fire chief tells me he found a body under the rubble of that building. I'd like you to take a look at it and see if it's one of the guys you came here for."

Bolan followed the shorter man through the crowd, stepping through the phalanx of fire hoses that formed another line of demarcation between spectators and professionals. The charred remains of the fire clogged his nose, wiping away the fresh salt odor rolling in off the sea.

"You've got quite a crowd on hand tonight, Sergeant," Bolan said as they worked their way around the smoldering foundation to a small cluster of yellow-slickered firemen.

"Yeah, well, a fire in the area usually brings out the boat people. There's a lot of petroleum products around here and if a blaze gets away from the fire department, the oil and gas could explode and spread a wave of flames right across the ocean."

"You sound like a man who's seen that happen."

"My daddy kept a fishing boat out here until he died. I guess that's one of the reasons I transferred out this way when I had the chance." He took another puff on the cigar. "A crowd this big also makes you wonder if the guy who did this is hanging around out there somewhere to admire his handiwork. I've got a couple of plainclothes guys working the crowd right now looking for somebody who might stand out from the rest of the people."

"If this does tie into what I think it does," Bolan said, "I doubt your men will find the guy responsible for the fire."

"Care to illuminate the cryptic statement, Mr. Belasko?"

Bolan grinned. "Not until I get a look at this body."

The small circle of firemen made room for Bolan and the homicide sergeant as they came closer. The sharp, sweet smell of burned flesh overrode the odor of wet, charred wood. The body had been partially protected by the same fallen timbers that had trapped the man. Both legs were charred to the bone, with a new polyester skin melted over them; the face was flushed as if from a recent sunburn.

"Is he one of yours?" Dansby asked.

Bolan nodded. "Jernigan, Robert L."

The detective reached inside his windbreaker and produced a notepad, making brief notations. "Care to tell me what this is all about now?"

Standing, Bolan handed Dansby a card with Hal Brognola's name and office number on it. "Can't. But if you give that man a call, he'll give you what the department can release."

An angry look filled Dansby's face. "Shit. That doesn't do me any good if I don't know who we're supposed to be looking for. Whoever set this building on fire could burn plenty more before I even find out what he looks like."

"I don't know what the guy looks like, either," Bolan said. "I know a few of the people he's looking for, but I don't know why. One thing I think you can be sure of is that the battlefield has moved on out of your town."

"Battlefield?" Dansby echoed. "You make this sound like some kind of war."

"Sure looks like it to me," one of the fireman observed, looking down at the partially burned corpse.

The fire marshal tipped his hat back and wiped perspiration from his thin, leathery face. "This blaze wasn't started from combustibles, Sergeant. I've got a man over there sifting through ash who tells me somebody firebombed this place with a high-explosive grenade. And Herschel oughta know because he did the same thing for the Army."

Dansby eyed Bolan. "You think that's what this was all about, Belasko? Some kind of drug war?"

"I'm sure drugs weren't involved," Bolan said. "But, yeah, this place was a battlefield for one brief moment tonight. And if war hadn't already been declared, you can be sure as hell it has now."

Dansby looked like a man who had a lot more questions, but Bolan moved on before the guy got around to asking. The trail was hot now. He'd arrived only minutes after Innis and his team had been hit. When he'd first heard it over the radio, he'd been sure of what the act meant. Jernigan's corpse only confirmed those suspicions.

So now the war was moving on, turning back in the only direction it had left to go: back to the beginning. It was what the stalker had contrived to do from the start of his killing spree.

Bolan stepped through the crowd thronged around the front of the Cherokee and opened the driver's door. A shadow separated itself from the others nearby, bringing a right hand up that glinted dull metallic.

Reacting instantly, the Executioner caught the shadow by the lapels of its jacket and swung it violently into the side of the Cherokee. A silencer-equipped 9 mm dropped from stunned fingers.

Bolan dropped his attacker with a knee to the groin that elicited a howl of pain. Stretching the man out on the ground before him, Bolan retrieved the dropped pistol and tossed it inside the Cherokee, bringing his own Beretta into view. He searched his prisoner's pockets, holding the man down with the barrel of the 93-R against the guy's throat. The ID belonged to a CIA agent.

"Who sent you?" Bolan demanded, easing some of the pressure off the man's throat.

The man licked blood from his upper lip and shook his head. "I was just told to carry a message to you."

Bolan thumbed the hammer back on the Beretta. "Who?" His voice held the chill of winter and the stillness of the grave.

"Hacker. He said you'd know his name. My section chief told me to tell you Hacker. I don't even know the guy."

"What was the message?"

"Hacker wants you out of whatever you're working on. He said he wants you to know that he's aware of who you really are."

"Then he knows I don't make deals," Bolan said. He thumbed the hammer down on the Beretta and tucked it away. "Take a message back for me. Tell Hacker the answer is no, and he should have known that before he sent anyone to tell me. Tell him I've got a copy of the fingerprints of the man who tried to kill me in San Francisco and that I can have Justice people start asking all kinds of embarrassing questions about why a CIA agent would attempt to shoot me. You can also tell him I have the file on the Hawks, and I'm ready to go public with it if I have to in order to keep him off my back. Make sure he knows that if anything happens to Greg Bowen while I'm gone, I'll do the same thing. Tell him I'm going to cut our losses on this operation and *he's* to stay out of it. You copy that, soldier?"

The CIA man nodded.

Bolan released the man's lapels and let him fall back, ignoring the uniformed policemen making their way through the crowd. He switched on the ignition and backed the Cherokee out into the street, heading for the airport. He reached for the mobile phone to get Brognola to initiate the arrangements necessary to get him transportation to Cambodia and the ordnance he would need once he arrived.

It was just as he'd told Dansby: there *was* a war on.

And the Executioner was going to help define and contain the hellzone.

12

Shane Innis squinted against the hot morning sun, shading his face with an open palm. He was dressed in olive fatigues, like the rest of the team. Adjusting the round hat he wore, Innis peered up the sides of the valley overlooking the river their boat navigated. Trees lined the incline, spreading long branches out over the river. Innis was all too aware that the foliage provided adequate cover for a sniper. He smiled slightly, anticipating the moment his hunter would put in an appearance. He scratched the square bandage covering the back of his left hand absently, a reminder of the attack on the warehouse in Miami that had killed Jernigan less than twenty-four hours ago.

The team had arrived in Cambodia by helicopter from a neutral base in Laos early the previous night and had "liberated" the boat they currently manned from an unlucky fisherman and his family near Stung Treng; their bodies had been weighted with stones and flung into the river.

Stung Treng was fifteen kilometers behind them now, with Lomphat about sixty-five clicks more west along the San River. Though lightly manned, there was still a Cambodian government garrison at Lomphat that had a helicopter. Innis intended to own that helicopter when the time came to jump back to Laos. Once there, the team could make the best deal possible for the gold and get the hell into safe territory. Maybe Australia. Innis had often thought of Australia when things in South Africa and Angola had turned rocky and hard.

Perhaps this time he would make the trip, take a year or two off, make sure Hacker and his dogs weren't looking for the team anymore, then find another war. He might even take an interest in the drug trade. From the looks of things in Laos and in Miami, the industry was wide-open to a guy who could think on his feet. And the money definitely appeared to be within the right range.

He pushed aside the mosquito netting that hung from the canopy and studied the bushes and trees again. The muddy brown water of the slow-moving river swirled in the wake of the boat, which was constructed flat and shallow and had very little draw. But it was a good vessel for the watery terrain it covered. The gasoline engine chugged fitfully, backfiring noisily from time to time and scaring birds from the trees. Raynes had tinkered with it earlier, while Innis and the other men had worked to remove the gold bars from the cache they'd made near the crash site fifteen years ago.

Innis could still remember that frantic scramble to hide the gold after they'd been shot down in 1975. They'd headed north, away from American forces, because Innis had wanted to steer as clear of Hacker's spook squad as he could. There was still some question as to whether the plane had been brought down by North or South Vietnamese forces, but the question didn't matter. What was done was done.

And there was still some doing left.

Innis shifted, sliding the strap holding his AK-47 around a little so that the assault rifle came more easily to his hand. His hunter was out there somewhere. He had felt the man's eyes on him while they'd backpacked the gold to the flat-bottomed boat. Even with the team spread out, with the boat practically an invitation to be taken, the hunter had hung back.

It had taken Innis a little while to figure out the reason behind that. The only possibility was that the hunter wanted it all: the team and the gold. Maybe that made the hunter's reasons for tracking down the team a little more understandable.

How the hunter had known the team had been forced to leave the gold behind was another mystery. Hacker had known. At least that was what Judson had acknowledged. And Raynes, who had worked in Vietnam for Quot for a time, had heard rumors that other Vietnamese knew the gold have been left behind during the scramble to avoid the Khmer Rouge and the VC.

The deck of the boat rolled a little as Raynes guided the vessel into the center of the river, shuddering a little as it pulled into a more forceful flow of water.

"Major?"

Innis turned and found Parker standing behind him. "Yes, Corporal?"

"Raynes thought he saw movement along the north ridge, sir. He wanted you to know."

Innis nodded. "Alert the other men."

"Yes, sir." Parker nodded and moved off.

Innis smiled at the salute the other man had given him just before turning to go. All of them were still so tightly bound to him, and they acknowledged the fact, still carrying his orders out to the letter without questioning. Hacker had known what he was forging in the jungles of Vietnam. Innis was certain the CIA man had forged small armies for private use before; and, perhaps, had had to deal with them the same way he had tried to deal with the Hawks at the end of the war.

Mad Dog.

Yeah, Hacker, as mad as hell. And this mad dog turned around and bit you on your fat ass. Innis closed his hand around the AK a little more tightly as the boat began a slow glide that would take them around a bend of the river. Trees grew in proliferation, obscuring the true lay of the land and what was on the other side of the bend.

His eyes searched the trees, skinning them free of their leaves as he checked for sniper positions. He stared into the bushes, waiting for the telltale gleam of sunlight on metal to give away an attacker's position.

Innis didn't notice the twine dipping into the muddy brown water of the river from either bank until it was too late. "Reverse engines!" he bellowed as he grabbed for a canopy strut, knowing what was surely going to follow. "Raynes! Reverse the goddamn engines! The river's mined!"

The first explosion ripped the starboard side of the prow, lifting the boat clear of the water for a moment, then dropping it back down. A wave of brown river water splashed across the deck of the vessel. Another explosion, closer to the port bank, ripped free huge chunks of mud and splattered it across the boat.

Innis fell to the deck, his assault rifle up and tracking for the hunter. The chatter of an automatic weapon opened up, but Innis couldn't identify the source because other members of the team returned fire almost immediately.

"Get that son of a bitch!" Innis ordered, cradling the AK in his arms. He hurled himself into the water to lead the way, diving as a stream of bullets hissed into the river near him. Blinded by the murk, he swam one-handed under the surface, clawing his way up the muddy bank to find cover.

Then he was blinking his eyes clear, marking the hunter's position somewhere near the top of the incline. He fell back into the bush, letting the jungle take care of him as it had so many times before. Now that the hunter had stepped out into the open the roles were about to be reversed.

Innis ran, anticipating the kill.

BOLAN FOCUSED the binoculars along the river again, taking care to make sure the sun didn't reflect from the lenses. It was enough that the helicopter ferrying him to his destination was following the path of the river as closely as it was without letting possible onlookers know binoculars were being used, as well.

Matt Smiley, an ex-Navy SEAL and sometime CIA agent Bolan had met on a recent mission to Ho Chi Minh City, piloted the small craft with an expert hand. Smiley had proven his worth and his loyalty during that mission and was doing so again. The big man had secured the weapons he and Bolan were going to use and had been waiting for the warrior just outside of Ho Chi Minh City when the Harrier dropped him off. He'd also captured the helicopter they were flying from a known drug smuggler who regularly shuttled drops between Ho Chi Minh City and bases in Laos. With the helicopter being known to the Cambodian government soldiers located in the sector Bolan was interested in, there would be less chance of the soft probe turning hard until the Executioner had located Innis and his team.

Bolan wore jungle camouflage fatigues, and his face was tiger-striped with combat cosmetics. An AK-47 rode beside his seat in the helicopter, muzzle pointing skyward.

Contrary to the Makarov pistol Smiley toted, Bolan had decided to keep the Beretta and Desert Eagle rather than use Com Bloc side arms. Both of them supplied superior firepower over the Makarov. And the firepower would prove more beneficial than something he'd pack in order to fit in with the locals when it came to confronting Innis and his team.

"Do you really think Innis got this far?" Smiley asked.

Bolan nodded, removing the binoculars from his aching eyes. He'd dropped into a fitful slumber while aboard the Harrier, but the rest he'd gotten had evaporated quickly during the past hours of searching and making their way carefully from Ho Chi Minh City. The delay in traveling from Vietnam to Cambodia had cost precious time that he wasn't sure could be made up. Opening his map case again, he rechecked the area he'd marked according to Kurtzman's files. It was possible that the Bear's intel had been wrong about the crash site, or that Innis and his team had moved the gold to some point farther than he'd estimated.

"The worst thing that could happen is that Innis has already been able to come and go. If I can defuse the situation here and now, lose it somewhere in this jungle, it'll be better than pursuing him through other countries where Hacker's men can reengage."

"Stay away from Hacker if you can," Smiley advised as he tipped the helicopter to assume a new bearing. "That man's pure poison, and he's got the touch of death."

"It's a little late for that," Bolan said dryly.

"Yeah, well, use it for later reference. I've heard the old man still has a few irons in the fire."

"Besides protecting the skeletons in the closet from Vietnam?"

"Yeah."

Bolan rubbed his eyes, watching the murky brown water swirl lazily beneath him. He felt drained by the trip, not anywhere near the peak of condition he needed to go up against someone as deadly as Shane Innis and the gang of cutthroats the man ramrodded. Those men were fighting for their lives now, knowing there was no possibility for a limited engagement or a partial loss. It was all or nothing. The greenery passed by under the helicopter, as serene in appearance as the river. But it was still the jungle; it nurtured the strong and ate the weak, as voracious in its appetite as any land-bound carnivore.

"I still feel responsible for that kid, Mack," Smiley said after a moment.

"Khoi isn't a child," Bolan said.

"No, I guess not. I don't think he ever knew the peace of a child's innocence." Smiley paused. "I should have seen this coming, though. He came to me years ago, just a skinny kid living in a world of hurt, trying to survive in a place that didn't want him. I did what I could and made sure he ate regular some of the time, but Khoi was hardheaded even then. He didn't know how to act around somebody who wasn't passing on guilt or slapping him when his mother wasn't looking. He would hang around my wife's village for a few days, then disappear for months."

Bolan shifted in his seat, focusing the binoculars again. He knew the story from earlier conversations with the big man, but knew Smiley had been filled with turmoil from the time he'd learned who Bolan was after.

"Khoi's uncle had never spared the guilt trips, either," Smiley went on. "It's a wonder that boy reached adulthood without some serious psychological hangups. It wasn't his fault that Innis and his men razed Khoi's grandfather's village during one of their 'unofficial' strikes against enemy camps and raped and disfigured Khoi's mother in the process. Yet Thieu dumped all that bad karma on Khoi from the time he was born."

Bolan said nothing, his mind filled with his own dark thoughts. Khoi had carried a burden for a long time, unable to rid himself of it. The Executioner knew about restitution; it was a major coin of the hellground realm where he lived.

"I tried to stop it a year ago when I found out Khoi had gone to work for Quot's men in the drug fields," Smiley said. "But before I could talk to him, Quot had taken the kid stateside. Khoi believed in the rumors that said the Hawks were still alive somewhere. He lived in the jungle and learned to fight, stole weapons and practiced, listened to every story anyone cared to tell about fighting. The times he seemed to enjoy most with me were when I told him about my experiences on the PBRs while still trying to win an unwinnable war under Uncle Sam's guidance." He paused. "I don't want to see Khoi die today."

"Neither do I," Bolan said. Something caught his attention in the distance, a twirling steamer of darkness on its way toward the blue sky. He lifted the binoculars and brought it into sharp relief. Smoke. "Down there."

Smiley nodded. "I see it. Hang on."

The helicopter dipped and changed course. Bolan cradled the AK in his arms after stowing the field glasses behind the seat.

Cresting a tree-covered ridge, the scene suddenly spread out before them. A fishing boat had listed into the riverbank on the port side, and men dressed in olive-colored fatigues were disappearing into the shrubbery. Even across the distance, with everything moving as fast as it was, Bolan recognized the men as Americans. The staccato banging of automatic weapons pierced even the beating of the helicopter blades overhead.

Smiley twisted the helicopter up and away as jacketed slugs ripped into the metal skin and spiderwebbed the Plexiglas bubble. The big pilot cursed vehemently, but the words were lost on Bolan as he ripped his headset off and prepared to leave the chopper.

There was no place nearby to set the bird down, so Smiley hovered over a clearing ten feet up. "I'll be back as soon as I can find a place to sit this bird down," he told Bolan.

The warrior nodded and slipped over the side, hanging by his fingertips from the skid for a moment before releasing his hold. Then he was dropping, loosening his body for a tuck and roll that would hopefully keep him from injury at least long enough to get him into the battle.

FROM HIS POSITION on the incline, Khoi stitched a line of 7.62 mm tumblers across the side of the fishing boat, watching the men on deck scatter. The mines he had jury-rigged across the river hadn't been as effective in disrupting the group as he'd hoped. They had reacted immediately, following Innis's lead into the river and up the incline toward him.

He stood, bringing the open sights of the AK squarely onto the man steering the boat. Raynes. Khoi remembered the name from one of the files he'd copied in Judson's house. The fishing boat rammed into the riverbank less than one hundred yards distant. Adjusting for the downward angle he'd be firing from, he set the sights at his target's crotch, ready to ride the recoil on full automatic.

Sporadic firing from Innis's team still raked the foliage around him, shredding leaves and chipping small branches from the parent trunks, but none of the men had seen him. Yet.

Bullets from Khoi's AK hit Raynes, zippering up his front, sending him over the side of the boat in staggering steps as they hammered into flesh. The body sank into the murky depths of the river, but Khoi didn't get the opportunity to make sure it stayed under. At least two of Innis's gunners had located his position and were throwing hot lead in his direction. Black dirt, plowed free by the seeking rounds of his attackers, kicked up into Khoi's face as he turned to flee.

A rock turned under his foot, twisting at his weakened leg, and he could feel the sticky warmth of the wound's pus rolling down his thigh. He suppressed a yelp of pain with clenched teeth as he regained his balance and dodged behind the thick bole of a tree, angling for higher ground.

Return fire arced into the tree behind him, scattering bark and wooden splinters in all directions. Khoi's leg felt stiff and unnatural as he forced it into a run. Panting, hurting, he reached for the anger that had sustained him for years. The anger, the need for destruction of the men now chasing him was a legacy Innis had left behind. It didn't matter which of them was ultimately his father. Perhaps he had already killed the man. All that mattered was that none of them left this battleground alive. It had to end here. He didn't know if he had the strength to pursue it any farther.

He recharged the AK and moved behind a boulder at the top of the ridge, taking cover. He held his breath, feeling the ache begin in his chest as his lungs demanded oxygen, and listened for his pursuers.

The men were starting to quiet down now, becoming more dangerous. They were at home, too, Khoi realized. The advantage of the chosen field was no longer truly his.

The jungle only allowed the growth and survival of the strong and the quick.

For a moment he felt lost, thinking he had only been a parasite in his years of living in the jungle. Innis and the others were predators who lived for the anticipation of the kill.

There had been no anticipation for Khoi. No sense of relief. There was neither now. Only the pressing need for some kind of absolution for the evil that had birthed his life, something to balance the scales.

Gritting his teeth against the pain in his leg and shoving the extraneous thought from his mind, Khoi leaned around the boulder and triggered several 3-round bursts at different spots of the incline. He saw one man hit the ground in a rolling dive then vanish from sight, but he was sure he hadn't wounded the man.

Stone chips flew from the top of the boulder as an unseen sniper rattled the trees with a sustained burst. As soon as the firing stopped, before the sharp echoes could fade, Khoi sprinted away, moving farther back into the jungle. Bullets searched after him as he ran, ducking below most of the branches.

A dark figure lunged into view to his left, caught in his peripheral vision. Khoi pivoted, dropping to his stomach as he brought the assault rifle into target acquisition. His finger touched the trigger and emptied the magazine into the man, sending him spinning away.

The thumping of rotors overhead caught his attention, and he watched the helicopter glide by only a little higher than the treetops. Someone was definitely interested in the action, but who?

Khoi tried to stand and felt his wounded leg buckle. Rolling over on his side, he pushed himself up on his good leg and lurched forward, fumbling in the ammo pouch at his waist for another clip for the AK. Before he could ram it home, powerful arms reached out for him, gathering him into a rough embrace that exposed his throat.

Cold, sharp metal rested lightly above his Adam's apple.

BRANCHES WHIPPED into Bolan's face as he dropped through the leafy canopy. The ground came up fast despite his readiness for the landing, and he almost sprawled across the mulchy loam before regaining his balance enough to turn the fall into a roll that brought him back to his feet. The sound of the helicopter had faded in the distance and the pops made by the assault rifles used by Innis and his team came to the forefront of the warrior's hearing.

Thoughts churned inside the warrior's head as he moved through the jungle, automatically taking advantage of everything the jungle had to offer in the way of camouflage. Thoughts of the untouchable CIA man, Hacker, of the sacrifice Greg Bowen had made toward the uncovering of the dark secrets believed dead and buried near this hellzone, of the deeds that had been commissioned of the Hawks to hasten American involvement in the war, and of the young man Matt Smiley had described who was running for his life somewhere in the familiar green hell that surrounded the Executioner.

According to the information that Kurtzman had retrieved, Innis couldn't have more than seven or eight men with him. The firing died away gradually, then the still silence was shattered by a sudden, long burst to Bolan's left. He dropped into a crouch, listening intently.

A rustle of clothing attracted the warrior's attention just before one of Innis's men stepped from behind the bole of a tree and lunged through the thick bushes at its base. Pale sunlight splintered against the brightness of the blade clenched in the man's fist, then it winked out of existence as the knife came slashing down.

Unable to bring the AK into play, Bolan stepped inside the lunge, slamming his body into the other man as he used the rifle to block the descending arm thrust. The man cursed as he tried to push himself away from the Executioner, snaking the blade toward Bolan again.

The warrior felt the electric kiss of the knife against his forearm, ignoring the sudden blood he felt spilling down his elbow as he smashed the butt of the assault rifle into his opponent's throat. The stock landed forcefully, cutting off the string of curses as it collapsed the trachea. Bolan fell on top of the body to keep the dying man from kicking and making his teammates aware that he'd been attacked.

The men were good, Bolan had to give them that. He hadn't even heard this one until the guy had made his move.

The warrior was breathing through his mouth from the exertion, trying to break free of the ethereal feeling that lay across the hellzone like a blanket. Perspiration ran down his face as his heartbeat became a background for his thoughts, almost becoming an audible sound in the silence of the jungle.

How many men were left?

He had no way of knowing. Innis would be the most dangerous one, though. Like the Executioner, Innis had traded one war for another, maintaining the same lifestyle, poised forever between one heartbeat and the next.

"Major!" someone yelled.

Bolan began tracking the voice instantly, angling up the ridge. He could smell the mold in the leafy carpet under his feet, and every nerve in his body seemed alive. Men's deaths were only a whisper away, perhaps even his own.

"Major, I got the sniper!"

Peering through the brush around the perimeter of the clearing, Bolan saw a young Vietnamese man he assumed was Khoi being held captive by a man he recognized from the Hawks' file. The man kept a knife tightly against Khoi's neck. Even from the ten-yard distance, the Executioner could see the desperate resolve filling Khoi's eyes and knew the man would risk death here and now rather than fall further into his enemy's hands.

Shouldering the AK-47, the Executioner paused in midbreath to draw the captor's face into target acquisition. He heard the running footsteps of approaching men cutting through the brush. Apparently Innis knew he was being stalked by only one man.

Khoi struggled slightly in his captor's hold, making it hard for Bolan to keep the targeted man in focus. It had to be a quick, clean kill, one that would impede motor movement and reflexes immediately. Otherwise Khoi would still end up with his throat slashed. A dark trickle of blood had already stained his neck.

The single shot cracked in the low-key noise of the clearing. Bolan rode the recoil, already searching for the approaching men. The 7.62 mm round tore through the man's forehead and threw the back of the man's skull across the foliage. The instant corpse fell to the ground. Khoi dropped to his knees immediately, groping for the assault rifle almost covered by the dead leaves and grass.

One of the men broke into the clearing and was starting to train his weapon on the Vietnamese man when the Executioner placed a trio of shots above his heart. The second man stitched a burst of autofire that chewed dirt in front of Bolan's position before the warrior's return fire blew a faceless corpse off its feet.

Bolan whirled in reaction to a faint noise behind him.

"Damn, but it does my heart good to see you work," Smiley said. He then proceeded into the clearing toward Khoi, who blinked dizzily at the sight of the big pilot approaching him with outstretched arms.

The Executioner maintained the integrity of the area as Smiley helped Khoi to his feet. Once he was sure Smiley had control of the situation, Bolan made his way to the top of the ridge cautiously, finding another dead man just on the other side of the clearing. That brought the total to five confirmed casualties.

The boat was still butted up against the riverbank. Bolan did a slow scan around the area, maintaining cover. Movement downriver attracted his attention. Squinting against the bright sunlight that separated the ridge from the extension of the jungle down below, Bolan made out the features of Major Shane Innis only a fleeting moment before the man vanished.

The Executioner stood and stripped off his gear, dropping the ordnance at his feet. The AK-47 went on top, followed by the webbing that usually carried the Beretta and the Desert Eagle. He kept only the Ka-bar, tucked inside his boot, and the big .44 in his right hand.

"You going somewhere?" Smiley asked as he helped Khoi up the ridge. His broad face held concern.

"Unfinished business."

"Innis?"

Bolan nodded.

"We could take the helicopter," Smiley suggested.

"No. If we've attracted the attention of any army patrols, you need to get the hell out of here."

"We aren't leaving without the gold," Khoi insisted in English. "It's part of my reason for pursuing these men. That gold belongs to the South Vietnamese people who are still trying to survive Communist oppression. It can do many things for the Meos and the Hmong—provide medicine, food and clothing." The look on the man's face suggested to Bolan that he would carry the gold bars out himself if he had to.

"Your call," Bolan said to Smiley.

The big man looked hesitant, then shrugged. "If you're sure you want to go after Innis on your own, we'll grab what we can off the boat and make a run for the border."

Bolan nodded. "I'm sure. You can take my gear with you?"

"Sure. Where do you want to meet?" Smiley asked.

"I'll find you."

"Lotta miles between here and there, guy."

Bolan grinned. "There usually are. But it's territory I've covered before, and I know my way."

"Good hunting," Khoi said.

Bolan nodded and moved out along the crest of the ridge, maintaining an easy lope, putting his mind into a mode that he was sure matched the thoughts running through Innis's head, locking his body into a physical rhythm that would eat up the distance.

Perspiration created a film that covered his body as the blood began to circulate faster, warming him from the inside out. After thirty minutes he could feel the muscles flagging, no longer carrying the buoyancy that had sustained him at the beginning. He was almost four miles from the river site where the fishing boat had been hit. Breathe, force it out, let it come in naturally. Maintain the rhythm.

The gap between the two men had narrowed to less than a quarter mile. The terrain had flattened out, making it easier to maintain visual contact. Bolan forced himself on, feeling the weight of the Desert Eagle drag at him, feeling the cooling sweet breath of the wind move against his body. His throat was dry, and the river was only a short distance away. He ignored his thirst, pushing himself into even greater effort, cutting even more off Innis's lead.

At a hundred yards apart, some of the lightness started to return to Bolan's limbs. Innis must have known the warrior was gaining, but didn't turn to use his pistol. Bolan wasn't sure if he could feel his feet inside his boots anymore. He was convinced if he tried to swallow, his throat would crack with the effort.

With less than fifty yards separating the men, Innis veered off course suddenly and headed for the river. Bolan mirrored the movement, watching as Innis came to a stop at the river's edge and sat down. He stopped upriver from the man, dropping to his knees twenty feet away, clenching the .44.

"You run well," Innis said after a few minutes. Sweat beaded his face and plastered his hair against his scalp.

"So do you," Bolan replied.

"You didn't try to shoot me."

"No."

Innis grinned. "You really think you can take me?"

"Yeah."

"A lot of guys have tried."

"I've taken a lot of guys."

"I suppose we both have. That's why we're still here."

Bolan didn't say anything.

"I was running for my life back there," Innis said. "What were you running for?"

"Because, at the time, I was the only one who could run after you."

"Why?"

"For all those people who never had the chance to run."

"For vengeance?"

"No. I've never even seen you before."

"Again—why?"

"Because I had to know it could be stopped."

"What?"

"Everything the CIA put into motion all those years ago."

"Meaning me?"

"Meaning you."

Innis was silent for a moment. "Then you should be faulting the CIA, not me. The Company made me what I am."

Bolan shook his head. "No, you made yourself what you are. The war allowed you to be everything that you wanted to be. I only fault the CIA for not stopping you."

"It tried."

"I know."

"Who was the guy who uncovered the team?"

"He could have been your son. His mother was gang-raped and left for dead by your team during the war."

"The sins of the fathers," Innis said.

"Something like that."

Innis tossed his Makarov into the mud with a soft splat of noise. "I'm not going to give myself up."

"I know."

Innis smiled. "Yeah, I suppose you did." He stood and walked into the river, stopping when it reached his waist.

Bolan laid the Desert Eagle carefully to one side and removed his boots, then waded into the water after Innis.

The merc feinted, then hit Bolan with a left uppercut that sent spiraling comets through the Executioner's vision. Bolan struggled against the other man, meeting and returning blows that staggered each of them in turn. His breathing became ragged, worse than when he'd been running. The metallic taste of blood flooded his mouth from a cut on the inside of his cheek. He hit Innis with a right that rocked the other man's head.

A cut had opened up above Innis's left eye, and blood dripped over his brow. When Innis dragged a forearm across his eyes to clear his sight, Bolan punished him with two quick shots to the ribs. He circled Innis, hammering away and being hammered in turn, looking for openings, exploring possible weaknesses. Another blow split the cut over Innis's eye wider. Bolan's right eye was starting to swell from a split cheekbone, and he knew it wouldn't be long before it shut entirely. He threw his body from the water, directing a kick that caught Innis in the upper chest before the man could move. He was repelled in the opposite direction, fighting to regain his balance, knowing Innis had had his feet more firmly planted than he had believed.

With a bellow, Innis landed on top of the Executioner as he tried to keep his head up out of the murky river. Bolan shut off a spluttering intake of breath as Innis buried him in the water. The warrior grabbed the merc's legs, trying to break the hold Innis had around his waist. His vision was beginning to blacken around the edges from the lack of oxygen and his lungs burned. He jerked an elbow into Innis's kneecap and felt the cartilage give way. The man's cry of pain was muted, far away. The grip around his waist relaxed, suddenly, and he was free.

Bolan got his feet under him and exploded out of the water, sending a palm smashing upward under Innis's chin. The Executioner chopped again, pitting muscle against the other man rather than technique. Innis fell backward, losing his footing in the mud. Bolan gave the man no chance to recover. His hands locked around Innis's neck as the man's hands formed a necklace of strong flesh around his own. He shut the man's breath off, even though he couldn't breathe himself. Unable to get their footing, they slid under the surface of the river.

Bolan kept squeezing, kept being squeezed. His lungs felt close to bursting. Then the pressure around his throat gave way. Bolan forced himself to stay under longer, still maintaining his hold. Long seconds later Innis began struggling in his grip again, no longer trying to hurt and injure, striving only to find an escape. This time when the struggling stopped and the air bubbles jetted to the surface, Bolan was sure of the kill. He gripped Innis's body by the shirt and dragged the man out, for a moment doubting his ability to save himself much less the corpse.

The Executioner staggered to the riverbank, finding himself yards distant from where the fight began. He sank into a sitting position, exhausted from the sustained effort. An hour later, when twilight had begun, he found a spot higher up on the ridge and began digging a grave with sticks and a sharp stone. He thought maybe some of the spirits of those Innis had slain would sleep easier knowing the beast was truly laid to rest. At least he knew he would.

EPILOGUE

Bolan found Greg Bowen in a wheelchair in the hospital yard of Walter Reed. The CIA section chief sat in the sunlight, watching the other patients, still a man apart.

Bowen looked up at his approach and a smile sketched itself across his pallid face. "The prodigal son returns," he said in a weak, hoarse voice.

"It took a little longer this time," Bolan agreed.

"You had your friend Brognola worried."

"He's probably still worried. I stopped by here first. I'd heard you survived."

"To fight again?"

"Something like that."

Bowen looked away. "That's the closest I've ever come to dying, Belasko. I've had time to do a lot of thinking these past few days while they started pulling the tubes out of me. You know what I found out about myself that surprises me most?"

"No."

Bowen looked up again. "That I'd do it again if I had to. All of it." He laughed weakly. "And maybe I'll get the chance to do just that. The Agency has offered me my job back. Brognola did a little whispering in the right ears while I was convalescing."

"Are you going to take it?"

"It's a thankless job almost a hundred percent of the time," Bowen said. "Long hours, plenty of chances to get your ass shot off, lousy pay. A guy would have to be crazy to step back into something like that. But I guess you'd know all about that, wouldn't you?"

"It's the kind of job where you make your own perks, Greg. You learn early to devise a code of behavior you can live with that will carry you through most things, and you hold to that as tightly as you can. Nerve and guts have to take you through the rest. Most people never truly find out the length, breadth and depth of their souls because they never face trials like the one you've been through."

"So you think I'm lucky?"

A ghost of a smile hovered on Bolan's lips. "No, just seasoned. It's still a hard world out there, and it takes hard men to lead the meek. We can't afford to lose even one."

"I know."

"So when do you start back?"

"In a month, give or take a week. And you?"

"No later than tomorrow," Bolan replied, meaning it. It was a hard world as he'd said to the young CIA section chief, and it did take hard men. All the time.

GOLD
EAGLE